The Running Back's Forbidden Temptation

Copyright

Opening Quote

I was sitting there waiting in my room for you. You were waiting for me, too. And it makes me wonder, the older I get, will I get over it? It's been way too long for the times we missed. I didn't know then it would hurt like this, but I think the older I get, maybe I'll get over it. It's been way too long for the times we missed. I can't believe it still hurts like this. What was I waiting for? I should've taken less and given you more. I should've weathered the storm.

The Older I Get by Skillet

Chapter One

☾ Sloane ☾

I stare up at the beautiful man in front of me who is staring back at me with love sparking from his beautiful green eyes. The incredible being who just vowed to love me for all of our days. The one who just kissed me so deeply and passionately, I'll feel it in my soul for the rest of my life.

The rest of the day is filled with fun. I feel surrounded by love. Well, except for the fifteen-year-old who hates me and is glaring daggers. Brant has had a strong dislike for me ever since he met me. He's made sure to make it very clear that he has a mother, God rest her beautiful soul, and that he won't ever allow me to take her place in his life.

I'd never want that. I'd never attempt to replace Brant's mother in his life or Remy's, his father's, life. That bond is sacred, and she should always be honored, even though she's no longer with us. She was killed in a car accident nearly two years ago.

In the blink of an eye as I'm dancing in my new husband's arms, the scene suddenly changes. I'm no longer in my pristine white gown surrounded by Remy's brothers and family. Not mine. I have no family. I'm now curled on the floor cowering from the man of my dreams.

Only he's not of my dreams.

He's made of my nightmares…

☪ ☪ ☪

I jerk awake with a quiet squeak and grip the sheets underneath me. I expect my nails to dig into a soft mattress, but they don't. Instead, they dig into the makeshift bed Brant made out of cotton and some old sheets. When he first made it, it was pretty comfy. I was impressed. But the older it's gotten, the less comfortable it has become. It's almost as if it has deflated like a balloon.

It keeps me off the floor, though. That's all I really care about right now. The treehouse might be my place to hide, but the wooden floor isn't all that great to sleep on.

I don't have a choice, though. It's this or be screamed at, belittled, and hit by the devil incarnate himself, or leered at by his brother's. This treehouse has become my safe place. Remy doesn't know I come here. After a beating, he typically passes out. When he comes to, I'm always back where I belong. I have nowhere else to go. He knows that. He knows I'm chained to him.

"You're never going to get away from me, Sloane. You're all mine now. You know that, right?" Remy whispers in my ear as he sweats over me and pounds himself into me.

"Yes, sir," I whimper. I turn my head and close my eyes, willing for it all to be over, but it's never that simple. He never just lets me lie here while he takes what he wants from me, whether I'm a willing participant or not.

Closing my eyes was mistake number one. I feel his hand coming towards my face before I have a chance to apologize or react. It lands hard, making my eyes shoot open. I scream.

And that was mistake number two.

"You can't look at me while I'm fucking you?" Another slap. I cry, and crying is mistake number three. "You've just got to close your eyes and imagine someone else?" A punch that makes me scream once more. Mistake number four, and the one that causes Remy to lose complete

control. *"Fucking whore! Who are you letting fuck my pussy while I'm away? Huh?"* *More slaps and punches.*

"No one!" I scream again.

"Little slut! You think I don't know you're riding another cock while I'm away?" *Another punch, this one to my stomach. A slap to my head.*

And it's the slap to my head that makes me black out.

I sniffle and gingerly hug myself. I wish that was the first and last time he did that to me, but it wasn't. There were many times before, and many after. It just got worse in the span of just a few months. Ever since Brant went off to college.

Brant Remington is a star Running Back for Brystone Springs University. It's not that far away from home, but when he left, Brant hasn't come back, even though he's less than thirty minutes away. I can't really blame him. His Senior year of high school was probably the hardest of his life.

Brant took over Quarterback for his cousin, Xavier, at Brystone Springs high school when Xavier went to college. He's a year older than Brant. As soon as he took over the team, he went from being Remy's pride and joy, to being Remy's Golden Boy. That might not sound like such a terrible thing, but it meant far more pressure on Brant's shoulders.

Ironically, it was all of that extra bullshit that brought Brant and I closer. Since his father and I married, Brant and I had been working on our relationship. He started to hate me a little less and less. He even let me use his treehouse to escape the torment neither of us could stop. I hadn't been hit during that time, but Remy and his brothers spent a lot of time grabbing me or belittling me. Yelling and screaming at me.

Forcing himself on me.

By his Junior year, Brant and I were actually getting kind of close. He even defended me from his father a few times. When Remy passed out, Brant found me in the treehouse where I'd run, and we'd talk for a while before I forced myself to go back inside and face my fate.

The first time Brant found me in his treehouse was just after Remy and I argued. I was only with him for six months and felt like I'd crashed into an alternate universe. Brant hated me the second he met me, but I could work with that. I didn't expect that Remy would turn into the asshole he had become. I didn't think that as soon as he said 'I do' meant that I became a possession. One that he could treat and abuse in whatever way he saw fit.

Even still, when Brant was around, Remy's fists never met my face. The bruises were all in places I could easily hide them. My back, stomach, my ass, chest… And I knew my role. Never to tell a soul. I couldn't go to the police. How could I? Remy is the police. So are his brothers. Who was going to help me?

After Brant left for college, the berating, screaming, shoving, and hidden bruising only got worse. Suddenly, he didn't try to hide them anymore. He didn't have his son to hide them from, so what did he care? He knew when Brant called home I'd just lie and say everything was fine. Remy has me trained very well.

"Yeah! Fuck yeah!" Remy yells.

"I knew Prescott would run it!" one of his brothers says.

He has them and a few friends over to watch a big game. The Dallas Cowboys are playing the Minnesota Vikings. My job is to make sure the snacks and beer never get empty. It's coming up on half-time right now. Which means the barbecue wings, chili, and mini franks need to be finished. If they aren't, I'll be punished.

It'll start out with a beratement in the kitchen. His brothers will then taunt me. It'll all happen away from his friends. After everyone leaves and Brant is asleep, he'll quietly yell at me as he pushes me around. Then, he'll take off his belt and make me lay on the bed. If I make a sound while he's hitting my butt or back with it, I'll get hit or punched in the chest or stomach.

Unfortunately for me, I messed up. I'm always messing up somehow. I forgot to plug in the mini franks. They're still ice cold in the crock pot. My eyes widen, and I immediately start to panic. Especially when I hear everyone getting up.

I have no time to hide the fuck up before Remy walks into the kitchen laughing with one of his friends. I look at all of them frantically before doing the only thing I can. I stand in front of the crock pot housing the cold mini franks and plaster a smile on my face that I hope doesn't look as fake as it feels.

I watch as everyone grabs a plate and dishes up. I've had chips and dips out along with fruits and veggies since everyone has been here. There have meats and cheeses, but the main course is to be served when half-time hits. All the real foods that everyone loves. At least I got the pulled pork done. Maybe no one will miss the mini franks.

Of course, I've never been that lucky.

"Damn. I was sure lookin' forward to those famous barbecue mini dogs you make, Mrs. Remington," one of Remy's friends say to me.

I meet his eyes, frozen in my place, and pray to any God listening that the ground opens up and swallows me whole.

It doesn't. I didn't expect it to. No God ever listens to me. Why the hell should they start now?

"Oh... um... I... was just finishing them up. I can bring them out as soon as they're done." I hope with everything I am those words appease the cold eyes staring at me. I don't dare look at them for fear they'll shred me on the spot.

"Yes, ma'am. Thank ya," Remy's friend drawls.

One by one, they trickle back to the large den where the game is on an eighty-inch TV. The only one left is Remy. He's been gripping the counter in a death grip ever since he heard that the franks weren't done. His arms are as flexed as his entire body. He's readying himself for an attack.

"I specifically requested those, Sloane. Why the fuck aren't they out here with the rest of the food?" His eyes burn into my soul. I feel like they're tearing away my flesh.

I try not to cry as I look down. My arms wrap protectively around my middle. "I... f-forgot to plug it in...," I whisper.

In a flash, he's standing in front of me gripping my arms. "And why the hell did you do that, huh? Who've you been thinkin' about?" Remy growls.

My eyes immediately snap to his, and I shake my head. "No one! I swear! I -"

"Fucking bitch!" he hisses. "Why do you have to embarrass me like this, huh?" He slams me against the counter, but I know better than to scream and alert anyone to my distress, even though the pain shooting up my spine makes me want to shriek.

"I -"

"Shut-up!" he commands. His voice is low so no one can hear, but it holds the same power and venom as it would if he were screaming at me. "You knew -"

Someone clears their throat, making us both snap our heads towards the back door just off the kitchen. I swallow down a sense of relief when I see Brant standing there with his arms folded over his chest. His dark eyes are stormy, and he's leveled a heated glare at his father.

"Dad...," he growls. "Everything okay?"

Remy plasters a smile on his face and lets me go. "Son! Hell yeah! Dallas is winning. Sloane was just finishing up some stuff. Right, sweetie?" He looks back at me. He's grinning, but the challenge in his eyes daring me to tell Brant the truth is prevalent.

I nod. "Yes. Yeah. I'm... finishing up the barbecue mini franks." I glance at Brant, but I know he didn't buy it. His eyes haven't left his father, and his six-foot-two-inch muscular frame is tense. He flicks his eyes at me. He doesn't need to say anything. I know what he wants me to do.

I turn towards the stove and find a pan large enough to put the franks in. I turn the burner on as soon as I have them transferred into the pan. There are no words spoken by any of us, but I can feel the heat from the intensity of Brant's glare raising the temperature in the room.

Without another word, I turn away from the stove. With my head down, I hurry out of the kitchen and slip out the back door. Brant wants me to go to the treehouse. There are no windows in the kitchen, so I do just that, trusting that he's dealing with the mini franks and keeping his father's attention off me so I can escape to my safe place.

I don't know why or how Remy hasn't figured out where I go, but I'm grateful that he hasn't. I think it's because he knows I'm terrified of heights. He probably doesn't think I'd ever climb to the treehouse. Especially since it's so high in the air.

Whatever the reason, I've never been more thankful.

I can't help the tears running down my face. I bury my head in the pillows that Brant left out here. I make sure I'm cleaning the sheets and things, so they aren't dirty, but the pillows don't smell like Brant anymore now. When he was here, his scent was all around me. Soothing me. Making me feel safe.

I sniffle as Brant's fingers run through my hair. I grip the waistband of his jeans not caring at all that he's a seventeen-year-old. He's my anchor. He's the only one making sure I don't drown.

"I don't understand, Brant," I whisper after such a long period of time that I'm not certain my voice will even work anymore. It does, thankfully.

"I wish I had answers for you, Jersey. I wish I could magically snap my fingers and make it all stop." His arms hug me tighter.

I suck in a breath because it hurts, but I let it out slowly. I don't want him to know the true extent of what's happening. He may be my life raft in the choppy water, but he doesn't need to have his whole life destroyed by what's really happening behind closed doors. He protects me all the time. This is my way of protecting him. At least in some small and insignificant way.

His fingers tangle in my hair. I'll never tell him, but I love when he does that and tugs lightly. It grounds me. It helps me to know that I'm still breathing. That no matter what just happened, I'm still alive.

"I'm leaving soon…," he whispers after many more minutes pass.

I suck in a breath again, but for a different reason this time. "I know," I finally manage to choke out.

"You know our plan, Sloane. You know how to get me home if you need me and can't tell me."

I swallow hard as I bury my face in his chest. "I know…"

☪ ☪ ☪

I don't know how long ago I fell back to sleep, but I jerk awake at a sound. Disoriented, I blink a few times, trying to bring my mind back to myself. I'm still in the treehouse and… Oh no! Oh God, it's light!

"I thought I'd find you up here," a deep, growly voice says.

I whimper and sit up so quickly, my head spins. But I don't care. I scurry to the corner of the treehouse as far away from the entrance to it as I can possibly get. I cross my arms over myself, trying to protect myself as much as I can.

I'm trembling.

I don't know what's in store for me, but I doubt I'll survive it. Not this time.

I ran away…

…and he found me…

Chapter Two

☾ Brant ☾

"Think you'll be back for the party tonight?" my cousin and best friend, Xavier, asks me as I drive from Brystone Springs University to home.

The party he speaks of is to celebrate our most recent win. Xavier Remington is the star Quarterback of our team. I'm a Running Back. Our other cousins are also on the team. Just like high school, they call us the Dream Team. We're good, and we fucking know it. Our win against the Florida Gators only proves that. The Gators aren't the best of all teams in the college football league, but this year, they have a good record and even better team. Our win against them was a big one.

"I don't see why not," I say. "I'm only going to be here for a little while. Kinda missed it."

He chuckles. "Right, Brant. I know you don't miss the house, the town, or your dad. You miss her."

Fucker knows me far too well. I sigh. "It's not just that, though. You know why I feel like I need to make an appearance."

"Yeah. Yeah, I know." His teasing voice sobers quickly. "If you need anything, just call. Colt is working, but…" He trails off. Before I can respond, he speaks again. "Drake is on standby, too. One phone call, and Blade will be there in minutes."

I nod but realize he can't see me. I have my phone on speaker, not video chat. "I know." I let out a breath. "I'm pulling up now, man. I'll see ya later."

I hang up with him as I pull into the driveway of the place I've called home my entire life. It's a two-story, modern home with four bedrooms and three bathrooms. The lower level has a game room, a den, where my dad spends almost all of his time, an office, where he spends absolutely none of his time, a library, a living room, and a kitchen. There's a fully-furnished basement that holds another sitting area, it's where I spent a lot of my time before I moved to the dorms, and has a large pool in the spacious backyard.

I sit in my truck for a few minutes. The last time I was here, I almost came to blows with my old man. He married Sloane when I was fifteen. I wanted nothing at all to do with her then. I was pissed my dad was marrying so quickly after losing my mom. She was killed by a drunk driver only two years before. I was just starting to be able to navigate life without her when Sloane dropped into my world.

My dad was dating her for only three months before she had a ring on her pretty finger. And that was the day I met her. The day they got engaged. My dad never even told me he was seeing anyone. I blamed Sloane completely. I was pretty sure she was the one who wanted to keep it a secret from me. I resented her and didn't make her life with us easy at all. I made certain to be the biggest fucking asshole to her.

Turns out, my dad wasn't making it easy for her either. I needed to get away from him one day because he was drunk and wouldn't shut the fuck up with his criticism of my performance in a game. I didn't expect to find Sloane in my treehouse silently crying less than six months after they said their vows. Vows that were very easily breakable, just like she was. For the past three years, I watched the once vibrant and bubbly woman become something that neither she nor I recognize.

But it wasn't until the day I left and saw a bruise on her arm that I truly realized just how bad it was for her. I woke up to my dad screaming at her over something regarding his coffee being too hot. I got down the stairs just as he was stepping back after yelling in her face. Tears were rolling down her cheeks, but it was the shape of his hand on her arm that got me.

I've never been in a physical fight with my dad before, but I got in one that day. I shoved him so hard that he fell on his ass. I screamed at him just as loud as he did to her. I stood over him just as intimidatingly as he was doing to her. I got right in his face as he did to her.

My dad was so shocked that when he got up, he had tears in his eyes. He hugged her so lovingly for the longest time, he ended up late to work. As they stood in the kitchen, I watched all of the tension Sloane had been feeling just dissipate second by second. And as it happened, my heart broke more and more.

What she didn't know and still doesn't is that I've been slowly falling for her. At first, I thought it was some stupid, fucked up crush. I liked being the one who got to hug her when she cried and listen when she talked. I didn't care if the conversation we were having had to do with her dreams and aspirations, or the fucking argument she got into with my dad that day. I just liked that I got to be the one to listen to her.

All I cared about was that when I found her that first time in my treehouse, my place of peace that I shared with no one, not even my cousins, everything changed. It kept changing each day. My confusing crush turned into something far greater and stronger. As I got older, I liked that she not only came to me for comfort, but listened to me when I told her to do something. Like to go to the treehouse when my dad was drunk.

Eventually, I didn't even have to speak the command. I just gave her a look, and she knew exactly what I wanted. I grew to fucking love that I had a power over her that my dad didn't and never did. And not a power in any kind of a controlling or derogatory way. More the power to communicate with her with just my eyes. The power that she'd do what *I* wanted her to over whatever bullshit my dad wanted. That she trusted *me* enough to listen to me over him.

I even loved that when she shied away from hugging me, that she'd do it if I gave her just one look. The few months before I left for college, she'd stay in my arms for hours, and we'd just talk. Sometimes, we'd talk about nothing at all. Others, she'd regal me with her vast knowledge on WWII and volcanoes. I passed my history class my Senior year because of her.

14

I take a deep breath. I haven't been back here in months. I moved out the day after I graduated high school. I didn't want to be here because I needed to get a hold on my feelings. I thought if I stayed away, I could get them in check and get over it, but I should have listened to Xavier when he told me that would never work. My feelings only grew stronger, just as he said. Fuck, just like all of my cousins told me they would.

I scrub my hands down my face as I get out of my truck. I don't see my dad's Corvette around. Sloane's navy blue Ford Escape is in the garage, which is open, and my dad's white Mercedes is next to it. I never understood how the hell he could afford such nice cars and nice house on a cop's salary, but I also didn't complain. I had everything I've ever wanted growing up. Including the cherry red Ford F-150 that's my pride and joy.

Fuck, I've already got a headache and a hard on. Just because the Vette isn't here doesn't mean my old man isn't. I don't want to deal with him at all. I deal with him enough on the phone when I call to check in. But the thought that I'll get to see Sloane up close and in person has me hard as steel. When I check in, Sloane rarely gets to say much to me. She always tells me it's fine, but I know she's hiding things.

Especially lately.

The last time I called, which was last night, I called her phone. My dad is the one who answered. I didn't get to talk to her, but I could hear her sniffling in the background. My dad's voice had a rough and very drunk edge to it. Sloane texted me at three in the morning telling me it was okay. She knew I was worrying. She felt it. I didn't get the text until this morning when I woke up. It was after eight. Somehow, I'd fallen asleep. I'm not sure how, though, because I was trying to figure out what the fuck to do for most of the night. I knew something was wrong.

I tried to call her, but her phone went straight to voicemail. That's when I made the decision to come back here. I need to know she's okay. Of everything that I know he's put her through, I've never actually feared for her life, but I'm there now. Before I left, I told her that if she's ever in trouble and can't tell me, to shut her phone off. That would be our signal. It's how I would know she needs help.

I open the door a little shakily. I'm not sure what I'm going to walk into, but deep down I know it's going to be bad. It doesn't stop my heart from hoping for the best. And it's that hope that has me coiled for Sloane. I just might throw all caution to the wind and kiss her senseless.

"Dad?" I yell when I step inside. I close the door behind me and don't hear an answer.

I let out a breath as I walk further inside the house. My heart feels like it might beat right out of my chest. I contemplate calling Colton DeLise. He's Xavier's husband. They got married the summer between Xavier's Freshman and Sophomore year of college. Xavier is a year older than I am. He's nineteen. Colton is a cop with Brystone Springs Police Department. He's twice Xavier's age, but they make the perfect couple. I know Colton would be here in a heartbeat if I asked him to.

I stop dead in my tracks when I see the state of the living room. "Fuck…," I whisper to myself. I know instantly that the small shred of hope I was holding onto is pointless. My heart speeds up. "Oh fuck."

The TV is smashed. The table is upturned. The couch and chairs have all been slashed. The interior of both have been strewn all over the room. Glass picture frames litter the carpet. My eyes dart to the kitchen as I run towards it.

"Sloane!"

The kitchen is in no better shape. Plates and glasses have been smashed all over the place. Pots and pans are thrown everywhere. Everything that was once in the cupboards and pantry are all over the counters and floors. I look for Sloane. Thankfully, she's not hurt and bleeding on the floor, but it doesn't help.

"Sloane!" I yell at the top of my lungs. "Sloane! Where are you?"

I run from room to room only to find more chaos and destruction. No Sloane. My dad is nowhere to be found either. The pool chairs are thrown into the pool. The pool table in the game room is upturned.

I run up the stairs. "Sloane!" I yell again.

I'm sure most people would be screaming for their father, too, but not me. I know this is him. I know he did this. I just hope to fucking hell, I'm not too late. If I find her bleeding out somewhere, I'll kill my father myself and gladly spend the time rotting away behind bars.

I check every single room upstairs and only find that each one has been ransacked and destroyed, just as the rest of the house had.

But no Sloane.

"Jesus fuck. Sloane! Where are you, baby? Fuck, talk to me!"

I stand in the middle of their destroyed bedroom and catch sight of her phone smashed near a wall. I can hear the pounding of my heart in my ears. It's not a fighter jet. It's a whole fucking squad of them.

I shakily take out my phone. Maybe I need to call Drake after all. Maybe he can get ahold of Blade, his boyfriend. Blade is the president of our chapter of Viper's Venom. Viper's Venom is a huge motorcycle crew that could probably rule the whole damn nation if they wanted to. They're bigger than Hells Angels and twice as vicious. If anyone can help me right now, it would be Blade. My dad is just as much the police as Colton is. This might be something Colton needs to stay away from.

I'm just about to dial Drake when a thought occurs to me. "Shit. Treehouse." I don't know why I didn't think to look there when I saw the destruction in the backyard. I was so focused on Sloane, I didn't even see the treehouse before I was running to the next room.

I shove my phone back in my pocket and take off running once more. I sprint down the stairs and outside. As soon as I get to the treehouse, I start climbing. I'm trying to listen for any kind of sound alerting me she's there, but all I can hear is my own frantic breathing.

"Please, Sloane. Please fucking be here," I whisper. Seconds later, my head is popping through the floor of the treehouse, and I'm relieved as hell to see her. "I thought I'd find you up here," I rumble in relief. It takes only seconds for the relief to completely fade. I'm not expecting what I see. "Oh shit. Sloane, fuck."

She cowers in the furthest corner of the treehouse she can possibly get. She's crying and staring at me with such an immense level of fear, my racing heart shatters. I can see she's covered in bruises. Her face is swollen. Her lip is split. Dried blood coats it. Both of her eyes are almost swollen shut. Her arms have angry handprints on them that are red and just as bruised as her face. She's wearing shorts, and I can see that even her legs are bruised. Cut open.

She lets out a blood curdling scream before she does her best to fold herself into the tiniest ball. Her legs press against her chest, and her arms cover her head as she hides between her knees as much as she can. My five foot beauty has been beaten to within an inch of her life.

"Please! Please, Remy! I'm sorry! I'm so sorry! Please! Don't hurt me anymore! Please, Remy!" she screams and pleads.

I pull myself up the rest of the way. When I was a kid, this treehouse seemed enormous. Now, I'm almost six-feet-two. I'm a big guy. Muscular with broad shoulders. Even crouching, I make this treehouse look a lot smaller than it is.

"Sloane," I say a lot more calmly than I feel. "Sloane, it's me. Not him. Me. It's me, baby." I kneel and make my way to her inch by inch.

"Please… Please, no more…," she sobs. She's trembling uncontrollably. I know if I touch her, it's more than likely going to send her into fight or flight mode. I know I could just hold her against me as she flails and tries to get away, but I want her to come to me willingly and know she's safe.

"It's me, Jersey. Me. Brant. Look at me…," I coax soothingly. Forcing myself to be calm for her is slowing my heart down. I don't feel like I'm going to have a heart attack anymore, but I might still burn the fucking world to the ground over what my father did to her. "Come on, Jersey. It's me. Who else calls you Jersey?"

She takes deep gulps of air into her lungs as she sobs. "Br-Brant…?"

"Good girl. Brant. It's Brant, baby." I've never called her baby out loud before, but the word comes so naturally to me that I don't give a shit. She's mine. She's been mine for longer than I'm sure either of us care to admit, and it's time we both quit dancing around that fact.

Especially right now.

Still trembling, she launches herself at me. Fresh waves of sobs overcome her as she grips my shirt tightly in her small hands. I hold her way too thin frame against my body and lay down with her on my makeshift bed.

"I got you," I whisper. "Fuck, Sloane. Fuck, baby, I got you. I'm never letting you go again."

She cries even harder and grips my shirt tighter. So tight, I'm sure she could rip the fabric if she wanted to. I hug her as close and protectively as I possibly can. I whisper in her ear that she'll be okay over and over again, but I'm not sure if I'm saying it for her or me.

I fucked up when I decided to stay away. It was selfish as hell on my part because all I wanted to do was combat my feelings for her, my thirty-eight-year old angel. I didn't think about what would happen to her without me around to protect her. I never thought my dick of a dad would ever cross this line, but it doesn't matter now. None of it fucking matters because it's never happening again.

I'll make up for this. I was telling the honest to God truth when I told her I'm never letting her go again.

My dad will face the music for this even if it's the last thing I do.

Chapter Three

☾ Sloane ☾

(One Week Later)

I step out of the shower and wrap a towel around myself. I use another one to dry my long, chestnut colored hair and let out a long breath. With the towel wrapped around my hair, I slowly swipe my hand across the glass of the mirror and clear some condensation so I can see my reflection.

It's been a week since Remy's last attack. The bruises on my face have faded nicely. The ones on my arms, chest, and stomach are an ugly yellow, but I'm doing a lot better. Physically anyway. Emotionally is a whole other story. I haven't been able to sleep at all. The bags under my eyes are prevalent and dark. I can't close my eyes without seeing him.

Last I heard, Remy had been arrested and released. In order to avoid any kind of conflict with one of their own officers, Brystone Springs Police Department brought in the Sheriff's Department to make the arrest and lead the investigation into Remy's actions. Not to say the department isn't still investigating, but they're allowing the county to lead it.

Currently, Remy is on Administrative leave. He's not allowed to leave the house during the hours of eight in the morning and five in the evening. It doesn't make me feel any better because I doubt very seriously he's following those directions.

Thankfully, he doesn't know where I am. And even if he did, it's unlikely he'd ever get through the wall standing between me and him. A wall I never expected but am beyond grateful for. I've never felt safer.

Brant.

Brant showed up at the perfect time like some kind of an avenging angel or something. I'd hidden in the treehouse after Remy beat me. I heard Remy throwing things around the yard and destroying the house, but I never moved from the floor of the treehouse. I didn't make any sounds after I ran from him. When Brant showed up that morning after he couldn't get ahold of me, I thought it was Remy. It took me time to realize I was safe.

Safe with Brant.

He only allowed me to lay with him a few minutes before he was taking me away from my prison. My own personal hell. He helped me pack my things. I don't have a lot. He put everything I own into his truck. He made a phone call he refused to elaborate on.

Few words were said before he had me at the hospital being checked out. His cousin's, Xavier's, husband, Colton, met us at the hospital. It was a whirlwind of questions. Photographs were taken. Before I knew really what was happening, it was all over, and I was being settled at Brant's off-campus house that he shares with a couple of his other cousins, Drake, Sterling, and Kody.

Drake gave up his room. He spends most of his time at his boyfriend's house. When he has early football practice or an early class, he stays on the couch downstairs. I feel awful I've displaced him and have tried several times to tell him I'm happy to be on the couch. Every single one of the guys tell me that's not happening; that I need my privacy.

Considering they're all football players, I'm shocked the house is so quiet. I'd think they'd all have women here all of the time. Parties. I figured it would be constantly messy, but it's not. They all treat this place like it's a sanctuary. They don't even let me do a lot of cleaning or cooking. They pick up after themselves and cook for themselves, too. They aren't typical college kids. They're incredibly protective. If they have practice or class and are all gone at the same time, they have one of their friends here so I'm not alone.

What throws me the most, though, is that they all treat me like I'm one of them, even though I'm nearly twenty years older than they are. They don't treat me like some kind of a mom, though. It's like I'm a friend. I've gotten to feel so comfortable around them. I don't hesitate to say anything or sit down and watch a movie with them. I don't even think about age. Everything is easy with them.

Everyone but Brant.

Since the day he took me here, he's avoided me like the plague. I don't know where he sleeps at night, but it's not here. I never see him unless he comes by to get something. It's almost like we've somehow reverted back to when we first met each other. Only this time, it actually hurts. I want him around. I love being with him. I love him just being near me.

My cheeks burn hot as tears sting my eyes when I think of him staying with some girl or something. I have no right to be jealous, but I know that's what I'm feeling. I hate the thought of him with someone else. The issue is that he's not mine. He never has been or will be no matter how he makes me feel. And how he makes me feel is unlike anything anyone has ever made me feel. He makes me feel special. When I'm with him, I'm the only person who matters.

"I'm so stupid," I whisper to myself.

I don't even know when I started developing feelings for Brant, but it happened. One day, after Remy had finished tearing me down, I was close to giving up. But then, suddenly, Brant was there. He sat with me and just talked about his day at practice..

I relished in the comfort he showed me. Days like that became more and more frequent, but instead of just sitting next to me, he'd wrap his arm around me. Then, it turned into him holding me close. Not just hugging me. I started dreaming of how things would be if he were older. How it would feel if I didn't have to stop at just hugging him. I slowly started realizing that I felt more than just gratitude towards him. I was seeing him in a new light. One I had never considered before.

I was slowly falling for him.

I found myself craving the stolen moments I got with him. I loved the looks he gave me. Most of the time, he didn't even have to say

22

anything. All he needed to was look at me, and he had me doing whatever he wanted me to. And I trusted that if his command went against Remy's, Brant would keep me safe.

And he did.

He did until the day he left for college. He promised he'd still be around for me, though. He called every night. We even had a deal that if I needed him and couldn't tell him that I did, to just shut my phone off. It was like our secret little signal. As dumb as it was, I loved it so much. Brant was like my superhero. The only one who could fly me to the moon and back; make me believe I could touch all of my hopes and dreams that he'd hung on the stars.

I suppose that all came crashing down in an epic storm the day Remy laid his hands on me the first time after Brant left. It's not like he hadn't before, but never like that. It was the first day Brant wasn't there to stop him from all of his depraved fantasies and violent tendencies.

I shake my head as a lump forms in my throat. I refuse to shed any more tears. It's all I've been doing for a week. I let out a breath and quickly brush my teeth. When I finish, I hurry from the bathroom towards my bedroom. It's four in the morning on a Saturday. They have a home game today. Their coach wants to get a last practice in, so they'll all be waking up soon to shower and eat. I really wanted to surprise them all and cook them breakfast as a thank you for this whole week. It's meant the world to me that everyone has been here for me through all of this.

I swing the door open and squeak as I hit something hard. I bounce off it and try to catch myself so I don't sprawl across the floor. Before I fully understand what's happening, I suddenly feel a cold draft hit my body just before I hit the carpet and do exactly what I didn't want to. Fall face first in starfish form.

"Ack!" I squeak.

Fully embarrassed, I scramble to my feet and realize far too late that I'm completely naked. Brant is holding my towel with a horrified expression on his handsome face. His deep brown eyes are wide with the same surprise I feel. My eyes widen so far that I'm certain my whole face is nothing but my eyes. I do my best to cover my chest and very much exposed pussy as I stare at him.

As if the universe has it out for me, I hear a click behind me. I know someone is opening a door, but I can't move. I'm frozen in place, and someone is about to see my naked ass. Brant's eyes flick over my shoulder and get impossibly wider. Quick as a flash, he grabs my arm and pulls me in front of him as he's spinning me. He propels me towards his bedroom and pushes me inside quickly closing the door behind him.

"Fuck, Sloane," Brant hisses. "What the fuck are you doing?"

"I w-was... sh-shower... I..." I wrap my arms around myself again as I stammer and stare at him.

The heat in his gaze sends shivers all over my body ending directly at my core. I've never felt so exposed while at the same time wishing for him to touch me everywhere. To make me burst into flames for him. Even in the dark, there's just enough light from the streetlights to see his eyes making their way up and down my body. It's wrong, isn't it? Why does it feel so right?

Both of our breathing is shallow, yet heavy. We're trying to control it but just can't seem to. His body is tense. I can see the rigid outline of his dick in his jeans. I try to look away, but it's impossible. Brant is mouthwatering.

Breaking the spell, he lets out a breath and thrusts the towel he's still holding at me. "I'm sorry, Sloane," he grumbles.

I snatch the towel and quickly wrap it around myself as he looks down. "Don't worry about it," I say just barely above a whisper.

I silently berate myself for all of the things I was just thinking. I know better. I've never considered Brant my son. He's never considered me his mother. We grew a friendship over the years, but nothing more. It's all it can ever be. Brant is nineteen-years-old. I'm thirty-eight, literally twice his age. He has his whole life ahead of him. Mine is half over.

I run a hand over my face and hurry towards his bedroom door, but he stops me. "Sloane, wait."

I shake my head. "It's fine. Really."

"No. It's not fine. I'm sorry I haven't been around." He looks down at me, but I refuse to meet his eyes. He cups my chin in his large hand, and I suck in a breath when he forces me to look at him. "I've been avoiding being here, and I'm sorry. You've needed me, and I resorted right back to treating you like shit."

I shake my head and push him back gently. "I don't expect anything from you, Brant. You have other obligations. You don't owe me anything." I reach for the door again.

"We need to talk." He steps in front of me again, this time taking my hand. Leaving no room for argument, he starts tugging me towards his bed.

I dig my heels into the soft carpet under my feet and pull back. "I have to get dressed. You don't owe me an explanation. You owe me nothing."

He lets out a sigh and turns on me without releasing my hand. "Sloane, enough. We've both been fighting this for too fucking long. It needs to stop." He tugs me closer and wraps his arms around me. "We've avoided this talk because we've both been too fucking scared to face it. I can't do this anymore."

I just stare at him. I want to pull away. I want to ask what he's talking about. I want to pinch myself and see if I'm dreaming. Of course, I don't do any of that. Instead, I shake my head and push away again, harder this time. I run for the door because I don't know what else to do. He can't possibly be saying what I think he is. I'm not worth that. I'm not anywhere near his league. I'm sure when the newness of fucking an older woman wears off, he'll probably run for the hills anyway.

I don't want that.

I survived Remy, but I can't survive Brant walking away from me. He means so much to me, and I just realized it right now. He's more than just my comfort. I'm more than just in love with him.

Brant is everything. He's my world. Not having him in my life would destroy me.

I shake my head when I reach the door. "This… we…" I yank open the door preparing to flee, but he catches me.

Once more, I find myself being spun around in his arms. "Fuck it, Sloane. I'm done. I'm not being good anymore. I want you. I want to show you the whole fucking world just like Aladdin does in your favorite movie."

"Brant…"

"Shut up, Sloane. Just stop talking." He lifts me as he slams his door. Seconds later, my back is against the cool wood, and his mouth is on mine.

As if my body has a mind of its own, my fingers are in his short, soft, dark brown hair. His stubble tickles me as he pummels my mouth with his. My legs automatically wrap around his waist. His hard, jean clad length grinds against my naked heat. I gasp and press myself against him harder. He takes my slightly parted lips as an invitation to dive into my mouth with his tongue.

Holding on for dear life, I grip his shoulders and close my eyes. My entire body sparks to life as I submit to him, allowing him to give me the best kiss of my life.

Chapter Four

☪ Brant ☪

She tastes even better than I dreamed. She feels even better against me than I thought she would. I've had her in my arms before, but never like this. Though, I've wanted this for longer than I care to fucking admit.

As I fuck her mouth with my tongue, her naked pussy presses against the zipper of my jeans. My cock is straining to break free and plunge inside her, but she feels way too good against me like this. I kiss her deeper and press against her harder, giving her the friction she obviously needs. I suck on her tongue and swallow her moans.

"Fuck, Sloane. I've wanted this for so long." I grip her ass even harder and pull her into me as I thrust against her.

"Brant, I'm -"

"I know, baby. Come for me." I kiss down her jaw to her neck. Not giving her a chance to argue with me, I keep her pinned between me and the door. I suck on her neck and nip lightly as I reach between us and start rubbing her clit.

Sloane throws her head back as she starts panting. She rubs her pretty pussy against my jeans, making me harder than granite. I rub her clit faster, giving her just enough pressure to make her thighs tremble and send her over the edge.

"Brant!" Her nails dig into my shoulders as she shatters, soaking the front of my jeans and making me want to follow her. By the grace of God or Satan himself, I manage to hold back. Her eyes fall closed as she moans my name over and over again.

I slow my rubbing as she comes down and cover her mouth with my lips once more. She opens willingly for me and kisses me just as passionately as I am her. It's like the two of us are pouring months of pent up sexual frustration for each other into the kiss.

She lets her head fall back onto my shoulder as she whimpers while she catches her breath. It takes her a few minutes before she finally dares to move. When she does, it's only to look at me.

"Where did that come from?" she whispers.

I chuckle and take a step back, still keeping her in my arms. "I've wanted to do that and a lot more to you for a long time, Sloane. You had to have known. I didn't try and hide it as well as I could've." I sit down on my bed with her still wrapped around me. The sun is just beginning to lighten the sky slightly. I can see the beautiful flush on her cheeks as she looks down.

"I didn't know you felt like I did." She keeps her eyes on my stomach.

I reach up and tug the towel she has wrapped around her hair. The only reason it didn't fall out is because of how tight it's wrapped around her. Her long locks fall free and cascade down her back as I toss the towel on the floor.

"I've learned over the past week that I gave a lot of obvious signs. Xavier was nice enough to point them out in the most assholish of ways, but I realized he was right. Here I was thinking I did a good job of hiding my feelings for you. Turns out, I did one piss poor job of that. The one thing I did do very well, though, was make you feel like you didn't matter to me when you were *all* that mattered. I never should've left you, Sloane. I'm so fucking sorry."

"You were at Xavier's…?" she asks softly, biting her lip. She still keeps her eyes down.

I run my fingers through her hair and tug. "Yes. Where did you think I was?"

28

"Your girlfriend's."

I can barely hear the words. They were said without hesitation, and it fucking stings. "Sloane, I haven't thought of being with another girl in almost two years." I tug her hair hard enough that it forces her to look up at me. I kiss her softly on the lips when she does. "I've gotten off to thoughts of you a lot, though."

She blushes and hides in my neck. "That can't be true. Brant, this is so wrong, isn't it? Are we crazy? Am I for -"

"Honey, stop that."

She shakes her head. "I'm married. I don't deserve you. You're so much younger. What if you get sick of me? I'm close to forty! I'm not your type. I'm -"

I slap her firm ass hard with a low growl against her neck. It's not the first time I've swatted her ass when her head has gotten in the way of her logic. Seeing her when I found her, I'm sure my father has done it, but not like I do. I do it to get her attention, but I know it turns her on. She knows instinctively that I'd never hurt her. It's one of the things I've fallen so fucking in love with.

I rub her ass lightly when she lets out a sexy little gasp just like she always does when my hand is on her pretty little bottom. "Stop it," I warn in a dominant tone I reserve only for her. "Your head is getting so far away from you, baby. I know my dad fucked you up, but you know better than that. You're beautiful, and I've never given a shit about your age. You deserve the entire fucking world. And as for you being married, you know fuck well that was over a long time ago. All we need to do is get you a lawyer and serve him with the papers."

She shakes her head, and I can feel her start slipping from me. She shifts and tries to pull away, but I know her far better than she obviously thinks I do. I hold her tighter and lie down with her. I grip her as tightly as I can.

"Brant, it's not that easy. I -"

"Enough," I rumble once more. "I know you think this is going to be a fight. Fuck, it probably will be, but you're not alone. And you sure as hell aren't going to be forced back into his house. You don't belong there. You belong with me, and now that I've had a taste of you, I'm not letting you go, baby. You've been mine ever since the first day I found you in my

29

treehouse. I protect what's mine just as fiercely as I love what's mine. And you're fucking mine. Got it?"

She doesn't answer right away, but I feel her grip tighten on the waistband of my jeans. I let my hand slide down her side to her hip. I grip her bare ass underneath her towel. Sloane settles closer to me like she was meant to be in my arms. It took me this long to truly see it, but she fucking is meant to be with me.

When I got her settled in the house I share with my cousins, I got scared and took off again. I stayed with Xavier and Colton for a week under the guise of keeping an eye on my father. Of course, they both know my ass well enough to know it wasn't that at all. I was running away because it's how I deal with my problems. I run from them. It's easier than facing them. Especially when the problem is a gorgeous, five-foot-nothing woman with haunting blue eyes and a fuckable mouth.

Thankfully, the two of them made me realize that running away from her isn't going to solve anything. I told her in that treehouse that I was never letting her out of my arms again. The first chance I got, I let her down. Running away from my feelings for her isn't going to make them go away. It only makes me yearn for her more.

"Come to my game today," I say after spending several minutes just holding her. "You haven't been to one since the playoff game in Xavier's senior year."

She stiffens in my arms, and I instantly regret putting that memory in her head. My dad spent the entire first half of the game berating her in front of his friends, brothers, and fans who didn't know her from Eve. She was embarrassed, but she did her best to stick around because I asked her to. She left at half-time in tears. I was making my way to say hi to her and to hug her because I needed to feel her in my arms.

She won't tell me what my dad said to her to make her flee like that, but I have my guesses. After the game was done and I'd gotten home, he was screaming about how much of a slut she was and how it would be better for her if she'd killed herself. He shut up instantly as soon as he saw me, and Sloane fled again.

My dad passed out on the couch. Sloane cried herself to sleep in the bathroom. She locked the door, but I begged her to unlock it. I told her I'd leave her be as long as she didn't keep it locked. I sat outside the door all night long protecting her and constantly checking on her. I didn't sleep a fucking wink. I never asked her to a game again. I always made sure to tell her I wished she'd been there but that I'd felt her presence.

Sloane lets out a breath and pushes me on my back. She straddles me, making me hiss, and tosses the towel wrapped around her, making my semi-hard dick hard once more. Her small hands find my belt, and she starts to undo it before I have any time to fully grasp what the hell is going on. When I do and have the presence of mind to grip her wrists, she's got my button undone and my zipper halfway down.

"Sloane, fuck. What are you doing?" I sit up, pinning her hands to her thighs. Her beautiful, perfect thighs that I have visions of being wrapped around my shoulders as she rides my tongue.

She blinks a few times, and I see the exact moment my words have the unintended effect of rejection on her. "Sorry…" She bites her lip.

I shake my head and smile. "Baby, the first time you make me come, we're going to have all night long." I kiss her softly when her eyes snap to mine. "I'm going to be buried so far inside you, you're not going to know where you end and I begin. I'm taking my time with you because one orgasm for either of us isn't going to be enough."

Her beautiful features light up even through the deep red her cheeks have become. Instead of saying anything, she hugs me, pressing herself fully against me. I can't help the groan that escapes from deep within as I wrap my arms around her.

"I'm… a little scared to go to your game," she says after several moments of me just holding her.

"Why?" I press a soft kiss against her neck.

She sighs and pushes herself up just enough so she's looking into my eyes. "Because he's not in jail. Remy is free."

"Not that I'm invalidating you, but you know you have nothing to worry about from him. Colton is going to be there. You can sit with him. So is Blade. No one is getting through those two."

She watches me for so long, I start to question if I fucked up somehow. Finally, though, she takes a breath and looks down. "Okay," she says softly.

My smile grows so wide, it could break my face. "Yeah? You'll come?"

She nods. "I'll come."

31

I briefly contemplate throwing out my own recently made up proclamation of taking my time with her and throw her on the bed so I can have my way with her before the game. What better way to get in the mood than by fucking the woman of my dreams before practice?

I somehow hold back, though, and kiss her instead. After sending her on her way to get ready, I hurriedly make my way to the shower. I know there's no way I'm making it through without rubbing one out.

After making a mess of the shower glass and cleaning up, I quickly get dressed, grab my stuff, and rush downstairs to the smell of something delectable. The guys are all sitting around the breakfast counter eating an array of food, but my girl is nowhere to be found.

"Where's Sloane?" I ask Drake.

"Don't know, man. She hasn't been down yet. Sterling made some oatmeal for everyone. I cut up some bananas and strawberries. Kody made some toast for us and a bagel for Sloane. I was about to go up and see if she's awake."

I don't say anything because I know he's covering for what he saw earlier. I'm grateful for it. Right before I pulled Sloane in front of me, Drake saw her in all that she wasn't wearing. While I wasn't at all happy that someone other than me saw her naked, I've never been more grateful that it was Drake who opened the door or that he decided to sleep on the couch in Sterling's room instead of downstairs. He only does it when he's tired and doesn't want to be bothered, but I've never been more thankful for it.

I grin in acknowledgement and change the subject. "Listen, I know Colt wants to come early with X and watch practice because he wants to take us to replenish our energy, but what's Blade doing?"

"He'll be there for the game. Why? What's up?"

I run a hand down my face as I sit down. "She's scared."

"Do you blame her?" Sterling asks as he sets a bowl in front of me filled with oatmeal and strawberries with bananas.

"How can I?" I dig in.

Kody sets a plate with toast and peanut butter next to my bowl. "I think if it makes her feel safe, Colt would probably have the whole damn police force at the game. I know Blade would be happy to set up his crew there."

"Fuck right, he would," Drake says. "Just need to make a phone call, and it's done."

I nod to him. "Make the call."

Drake grins. "You serious, bro? You finally admitting your feelings for Sloane after all this time?"

I smile, but I wince slightly. "I've really fucked up, haven't I?"

"Nah," Sterling says. He's a lot like Xavier in the fact that he's often the voice of reason. "Better late than never. The only thing you fucked up on is completely ignoring us when we told you not to leave her alone with him. We all knew something was fucked up."

I groan to myself and rub my temples as I close my eyes. "Never again. When your stupidity slaps you in the fucking dick, and you realize what a selfish prick you've been, it's a whole new world, let me tell you."

Drake chuckles. "I texted Blade. He's got some guys on Remy, but he'll pull everyone else if it makes her feel safe."

I open my eyes and go back to my breakfast. "Thanks, man."

"She's one of us now," Kody says. "You know what that means."

I nod because I do. It means she'll never be alone again. She'll never have to fight her battles by herself. She's got us next to her, and a whole damn army behind her.

The fucked up thing is that I know damn well that army is going to come into play sooner rather than later. If I've learned anything over this past week, it's that my dad has a side to him that no one really saw or expected. A side only Sloane knew.

A side that opened Pandora's Box into the secrets my dad hides behind. Secrets I haven't told anyone in this room yet.

Especially Sloane.

Chapter Five

☾ Sloane ☾

I clear my throat gently. I'm sure no one in the kitchen knows that I heard them say I'm a part of them now. I don't know why it soothes me to know that I'm a part of this group. They're so much younger than me, but it doesn't feel like that. I feel truly safe with them.

Just like I do with Brant.

"Hey, Sloane!" Sterling says with a grin when he spots me. He pushes a plate with a bagel and strawberry cream cheese on it towards Brant.

I smile as I take a deep breath and step into the kitchen. "Hi," I say softly.

Brant turns with a million-watt smile and shifts just enough so that when I reach him, he can easily pull me between his legs. I go willingly, but I know I'm blushing as red as a cooked lobster. I'm probably just as done, too. I know that the feelings I have for Brant are too far out of my grasp to ever be able to reel back in.

Brant's hand rests on my hip as he finishes his breakfast. I start eating my bagel, but I'm suddenly not all that hungry. I barely get a couple of bites in before Brant, the observant asshole he is, notices that something is off.

"What's up, baby?" he asks. His eyes aren't the only ones on me.

I sigh and look down because he's not the only observant one in this room. All of his cousins are, and it's as unnerving as it is endearing. "I guess I'm just more nervous than I thought about this game. Just being out there is really just scary for me."

Brant squeezes my hip and rubs his hand up and down my thigh. He kisses my shoulder softly and sweetly. "I promise he won't get to you at the football stadium."

"I have Blade bringing in some extra guys," Drake says to me. "And I texted X. He said Colton will be there. You know you're safe with him."

I bite my lip. "Am I, though?" I keep my attention focused on my bagel, even though I'm not eating it. "Even though he was nice to me, Colton is a cop, just as Remy is. I've learned quickly that cops stick with cops. They did with Remy."

"Well, there's a big difference," Kody starts. "The cops who stuck with Remy are all his friends. A couple are brothers. We know that the department is being hardcore cleaned up still. There's still some corruption being uncovered, but it's getting less and less. Colton isn't involved in that."

I shrug. "Or he is and he's just super good about playing the good guy."

Brant chuckles. "I know where this is coming from, but I'm going to ask you something. Do you trust the people in this room?"

There's no hesitation at all there. I nod my head. "Of course."

"What about me, Jersey?"

My eyes snap to his. "You know how much I trust you. I trust you with my life."

"Then trust me when I tell you that you can trust Colton. X wouldn't have married the guy if he was dirty. I don't care how good of a fuck the guy might be. Xavier has morals and standards."

I nod again and allow myself to breathe as I look back down at my plate. I force a few more bites because I know I need to eat. I eat like a bird. It's something my best friend told me in high school, and it's not something that's changed in the slightest.

I grew up in New Jersey. I moved to Brystone Springs after high school and went to college at the same university that Brant is. I've been in Texas twenty years. I've adopted the Southern accent, but I still have a Jersey twinge that I believe will never go away.

It's the reason Brant calls me Jersey. He's the only one who does, and I love it so much. No one else gets to call me Jersey. It's always been something special between us. Something no one else can have.

Brant kisses my bare arm as he growls low. "I fucking hate that he did this to you."

I look down at my arm and see the bruise from Remy's hand. "I... planned on wearing something that covers it," I say quietly.

"Then you're in luck." He reaches for something and hands it to me. It takes me a few minutes to realize that it's a jersey.

I furrow my brows and look at him. "What's this for?"

He grins. "You. Wear it. It's my jersey. It probably smells just like me." He smirks.

My hands seem to grow a mind of their own. They lift the jersey to my face. I close my eyes and inhale deeply. It does smell like him. Everything he is. Strong. Calm. Fresh. Spicy. Sexy. I open my eyes and just stare at him. I can feel everyone else look at us. I know they're smiling, but the only one I see is Brant.

"Don't you need it? For the game?" I ask quietly.

He shakes his head. "No. It's kind of like high school when the guy gives the girl his jersey to wear on game day to show support for him." He smirks again, but this time, the possession in his eyes makes me shiver. "And to show that the girl is his."

I bite my lip at the words and focus my full attention on putting it on. I love being his, but his admission makes me wet. I'm still struggling with what kind of person I am to have this kind of reaction to a man half my age. The more he touches me, looks at me, and talks to me, the less I find I care.

I look up at him when I get it on and blush at the possessive gleam in his eyes as he looks me up and down. No one has ever looked at me like him. Not even his father. None of my past boyfriends. Brant is the only one who has ever made me want to jump him with a single gaze while simultaneously making me feel like I'm the most important person in the world to him; that I really am his.

36

☪ ☪ ☪

I squeeze Brant's hand tight and try not to hyperventilate when I see Drake kissing a guy wearing a patch I know well. Viper's Venom. I've heard a lot about them from Remy, so seeing the President of the Texas Chapter of a very dangerous and ruthless motorcycle crew truly freaks me out.

I can't help but look up at Brant. I know my eyes are conveying the question I want to ask but can't over the fear. Brant's smile sets me at ease, but only slightly. I squeeze his hand tighter because my heart rate is spiking hard. I can't even form words to articulate the anxiety I feel right now. What have I gotten myself into? Was I a fool to trust any of these people? What's happening?

Brant leans down and kisses me. "Breathe, baby," he whispers against my lips. "Breathe."

I keep my terrified eyes on his calm ones and take a deep breath. I want to close my eyes to everything and focus completely on him, but I can't. "That's the VV...," I whisper. "He's the VV."

Brant glances in the direction of Drake and the intimidating man covered in tattoos with a dangerous glint in his smirk. He takes my other hand as he turns and steps in front of me, blocking everything out of my view but him.

He brings both of my hands to his lips and kisses them. "Do you trust me?" he asks, his lips brushing against my fingertips.

"Of course I trust you," I whisper, stepping closer to him.

He kisses my fingertips again, and I shiver. He puts my hands on his chest and smoothes his calloused fingers up my arms, leaving goosebumps in his wake. When he reaches my shoulders, he steps closer. His hands move down my back until they reach my butt. He pulls me as close to him as possible and kisses me long and deeply. My body melts against his, and my brain forgets all of the uncomfortableness I'd felt only moments ago.

He pulls away slowly. He lets his hands move up to the small of my back as he hugs me tightly against him. "Blade is the President of Viper's Venom. But everything you've heard about them from my dad is false. Their crew is totally legal. It's not like Hell's Angels. Their main guy is up in Chicago, and he's allied with some powerful people who are also on the up and up. I promise, Sloane. I'd never put you in harm's way. Blade would never hurt you. Think of him more as a protector. That's really what he is."

I wrap my arms around his waist and let him engulf me. It's one of the things I love so much about him. He's tall and muscular. I'm over a foot shorter than him and half his size. It doesn't take much for me to feel like I disappear from the world; that he's my protective shield.

"I trust you." My voice is stronger, but only because he gives me strength.

"Then trust me when I tell you that Blade will protect you from anything. He'll stand in front of a thousand bullets for you. Same as me and anyone else here. You have nothing to fear, Sloane." His voice is low and only for me to hear. His gentle tone melts my insides.

It takes such little time for me to fall a little deeper in love with him. Few words. Even less actions. I know I'm gone when it comes to him. I nod into his chest to let him know that I understand and really do trust him. He kisses my temple and takes my hand. He leads me to his group of friends and the biker. I hold his hand tight and stick close to him, my body half behind his.

"Blade, this is Sloane," Brant says with a grin. "She's a little shy."

I blush and hide further behind him, pressing my heated face into his arm. "Brant," I whisper.

Blade chuckles. "Hey, Sloane."

I peek out at him and take a deep breath as I let go of Brant's hand. I take his extended hand and shake it before immediately grabbing Brant's again. "Hi."

"Looks like you'll be hanging out with me and Colton," Blade says with a smile as he jerks his head in Colton's direction.

Colton's grin lights up his face. "Hey, Sloane. Nice to see you again."

"You, too," I say quietly.

"Alright, guys. We need to get our asses to the locker room before Coach kicks them," Xavier says.

I watch as Kody, Drake, and Sterling all jog after Xavier. Brant hangs back and tugs me from behind him. He cups my cheek and leans down. His lips graze mine. I squeeze my thighs together because just his lips have me wanting his tongue to make me lose control.

"If I had time," he whispers with a smirk and devilish glint in his gorgeous dark eyes as they zero in on my thighs.

I gasp and turn fifty shades of red. "Stop that." I can't help the giggle but cover my mouth with wide eyes as I look towards Colton and Blade. Thankfully, they're not paying attention.

Brant tangles his fingers in my hair and tugs until I'm looking up at him. "Be good."

I smile and lean into him. "Yes, sir," I whisper. I blush even darker at how natural saying those words feel. How I've only ever wanted to say them to him.

Something flashes in his eyes. Something a little dangerous and a lot dark. Something that calls to my soul. He leans in and kisses me so deeply, I feel like I'm floating. His tongue lashes against mine. The kiss is so powerful and more dominating than I've ever felt before. If he wasn't holding onto me, I'd fall to the ground at his feet.

He pulls slowly away. "Good girl," he says huskily. He taps my ass as he kisses my forehead before he jogs towards the locker room.

I let out a long breath as I hug myself and watch him jog away. His long, muscular frame looks so graceful.

"Ready to head in there, Sloane?" Colton asks, snapping me from my reverie.

I shake my head slightly to rid all of the sexy thoughts watching Brant's ass has put into my head. I walk towards them. "Yeah. I'm ready."

I follow them inside the stadium. There are a few people there, and that surprises me a little. I hadn't expected to see anyone else. I catch myself inadvertently stepping closer to both Colton and Blade. They lead me to a place close to the field and let me sit between them.

But my eyes still dart around.

Blade drops his arm over the back of my seat and points towards the entrance of the stadium. "See over there? That guy standing there?" For a tough ass biker, his voice is very calming. I nod. "That's one of my crew. No one is getting through him." He points towards the locker room entrance that we just came through. "And do you see those two guys?" He turns and points to several places around the stadium where men dressed in jeans, leather, and Viper's Venom patches all stand.

"I see them."

"They're all here for you."

"I know you have a strong distrust for Brystone PD right now, so Blade brought in his guys instead," Colton tells me. "They're all over. And when the game starts, they'll all be around you. No one is fucking with you, Sloane. No one is getting anywhere near you."

"They'll have to go through us and all of them before that happens."

I smile and relax more and more as the minutes go on. By the time the team is on the field for practice, I'm starting to feel a little more like myself again.

Chapter Six

☪ Brant ☪

(Two Weeks Later)

I can't wait anymore. I feel like it's been years since I've had my girl close. It's really only been a few hours. I had Sloane in my arms and my dick down her throat before my team took the field at our recent out of town game.

But it's not enough. It's never enough. I'll never be able to get my fill of her. Ever since that day in my room when she came against my cock while I was kissing her and rubbing her clit, we've both been insatiable. I've had her in every position imaginable.

Except one.

Sloane is shy, but my dad made my beautiful woman's self-esteem reach lows I never thought possible. She'll ride me with a fuck of a lot of coaxing, but she won't sit on my face. She won't let me eat her out. I don't know what he did to her, but she's terrified I won't like the way she looks while riding my tongue or the way she tastes.

I may be a very dominant person, and she may follow my lead and commands like the good girl she is, but that's her hard limit. A good dominant would never make his girl do what she doesn't want to or isn't comfortable with. But a really good dominant will do everything in his power to make his girl become more and more confident in her own skin. He'll help her to gain strength and push past her insecurities bit by bit. And he'll never leave her side the whole journey.

I push Sloane a little harder against the locker in the locker room my team is using. Well, were using. I'm sure everyone is out in the bus right now wondering where the fuck I am, but there are far more important things on my mind.

"Fuck, Sloane. Let me taste you...," I rumble against her lips right before I take them in a punishing kiss.

She smiles and lets out an adorable giggle. "You are tasting me..."

I can't help the grin as I swat her ass. She jumps with a squeak. "Sassy girl." I nip her lip as I pull away. "You know what I mean." I kiss down to her neck. "Let me taste that pussy you've let me fuck and claim as mine so many times."

Her breath hitches. She hasn't gotten used to my give-no-fucks mouth when it comes to her. She'd never admit it because of how shy and submissive she is, especially in the bedroom, but she loves when I talk dirty to her.

Her grip on my shoulders tightens. She tilts her neck to the side to give me more access to her soft skin. I let my teeth scrape lightly over her as her nails dig into my back. She presses herself closer to me and kisses my arm.

"Okay...," she whispers.

The smile that spreads across my face could probably provide enough light for the whole fucking city, but it's nothing compared to how hard she just made my dick. I take her hand and tug her towards a bench. She watches me curiously as I lay down.

"Come here, beautiful. Straddle me."

Her eyes go wide as saucers as her eyes dart around the locker room and towards the door. "Are you crazy?" she hisses as her eyes snap back to mine. "What if someone comes in?"

"Then they'll walk right back out. Now come here. Let me taste what's mine."

"Oh my fuck, Brant." She nervously runs her fingers through her hair as she glances around once more. Shakily, she finally does what I told her to. Only she's not close enough to my mouth.

I grip her hips and guide her towards my mouth. Her eyes keep looking around until I swat her ass with both hands then squeeze it. "I want your full attention."

Her eyes drop to me. "I'm sorry."

"Don't apologize, Jersey. Just say 'yes, sir' and do what you're told. Now, come here."

"Yes, sir," she whispers as she licks her lower lip. I groan because I love when she does that.

Sloane is wearing a pair of the tightest and sexiest jean cutoffs I've ever seen. If I hadn't watched her put them on this morning, I'd swear to fuck they were painted. I lean forward and kiss her stomach. She's also wearing my jersey, and I fucking love the way she looks in it.

Keeping one hand firmly on her ass, I drop the other to her leg and trail it up her silky skin. I love I'm always able to give her goosebumps. I love her soft sighs and sexy whimpers even more.

When I reach the crux between her thighs, I push her shorts and panties to the side exposing a beautifully waxed and very wet pussy. I'd tease her, but I can't wait. I need to taste her.

"Fuck me, you're beautiful." I swipe my tongue slowly from her heat to her tiny bundle of nerves. I know I've hit the right spot because she jerks her hips into me. She grips my arms for balance; lets her head fall back.

I do it again but slower. I pause at her clit and suck. She jerks into me again, but her eyes are still open. She still feels nervous to me, though, and I won't have that. I lick again and again, but I don't suck her clit into my mouth a second time, and I don't let my tongue slip into her pussy.

I pull her down a little more, though, so when she feels me suck and lick her, she also feels more pressure from my tongue. I know the more pressure she feels, the more the pleasure inside her will build. When she finally comes for me, it'll be powerful and satisfying for her and me. I love when I come inside her or when she swallows me, but I love even more when I get to give her pleasure.

She murmurs something I don't understand as she closes her eyes. I feel her relax into me more and more, and it's only then that I give her what she's silently begging for. I let my tongue dive inside her and thrust it hard.

"Oh, Brant... Fuck!" Her nails dig into my arms as she trembles and begins thrusting over my tongue.

And it's then that I ravish her. Using my whole mouth, tongue, and teeth, I lick, suck, and lightly scrape my teeth over her pussy. My tongue swirls just as much inside her as it does over her clit. I moan low and rumble again and again because I know the sound of my voice sends tremors of pleasure rippling through her.

"You taste just as sweet as you smell," I growl into her pussy. She jerks into my tongue before she finally gives in and lets go completely. She starts riding my tongue. Her hand spears my hair, and she tugs, pulling me closer to her sex.

"Yes... Brant! Brant!" Her thighs start trembling as her pussy clenches around my tongue. Her entire body feels like its humming with an energy only I can give her.

All for me.

Mine.

"Come for me, Jersey. Give me what I want. Let me taste that sweet pussy come."

Keeping one hand in my hair, the other slaps over her mouth as she screams. "Brant! Fuck!" Her body tenses right before she starts spilling into my mouth as her hips jerk over me.

I want to reach down and give myself a couple of strokes to ease the ache in my hard cock, but I don't. This was for her.

I lick her clean as she slowly comes down, panting and trembling. I'd give her all the time in the world, but before I can stop her, she's scrambling off me and righting her clothes. I lick my lips as I sit up and wipe my face on my shirt.

"Brant! Time to go, man!" Xavier says as he walks into the locker room. He takes one look at me before his eyes fall on Sloane. He grins as he backs out of the locker room. "Take your time, bro."

I shake my head with a small smirk. "He's a good guy, but he has no fucking chill."

"We should... I... should go... I'm sure Blade is waiting." She quickly darts for the door, but I'm a lot faster than she is.

I'm on my feet and have her in my arms with her back pinned against me in seconds. "Stop, Jersey. Get out of your head. I know your insecurities very well. We talked about this." I sway gently with her as she sniffles. I press my lips against her neck. "He has no power over you. No hold. You're a beautiful woman, and you taste fucking amazing. And once you get out of your head, let go, and enjoy things, you're that woman I know you are deep within."

She sniffles and nods, but she's shaking. I hug her tighter and hold her just like that until I know we can't stay in here any longer. I lead her to Blade's bike. He hands her a pair of jeans. She looks at him confused.

"They're gonna be too big, but it's gonna be chilly on the way back," he explains.

I hadn't thought about that, but I immediately take off my Brystone football hoodie as she puts on the jeans still not saying a word. Blade looks at me with a raised eyebrow. All I can do is give him a sad smile as I help her on the back of the bike after she puts my hoodie on.

"I'll see you soon, Jersey," I say with a soft kiss to her lips and a big hug.

"Yes, sir," she whispers.

It's the faint twinkle in her eyes that shows me she's not going to run from me. That I didn't blast through her boundaries and destroy her in the process. I know my girl. I know that, sometimes, she needs to work through things in her own way before she comes to terms with them.

As much as I hate myself for walking to the bus that's been waiting on me, I also know that this ride back to Brystone Springs without me is what she needs.

But while I watch her ride off with Blade and his crew, I have to shake off the feeling that she's not going to be there when I get back…

Chapter Seven

☪ Sloane ☪

"Mmm...," I groan. My eyes feel heavy. I try to open them, but they feel gritty. Like I'm trying to open them with my face buried in sand.

It's that thought that makes my eyes fly open. The blinding pain in my head forces them shut once more.

I lie as still as possible while I try and figure out where I am and what happened. It's cold and smells dank. I know I'm not home. I'm not in Brant's bed where I've spent every single night of the past couple of weeks wrapped in his arms. I'm definitely on something hard. Concrete, I think. It doesn't feel like an actual floor, hardwood or not. This is definitely different.

"Fuck," I whisper. I need to get my eyes open. I try to move my hands to rub my eyes, but they're tied to something.

The panic forces my eyes open again. I frantically try to get my hands free, but I can't. Ignoring the pain stabbing me in the back of the head, I crane my neck back and sideways to look more at my surroundings.

"Oh, God..." The panic moves from my chest straight to my brain.

I want to scream and try to get away, but I don't do any of that. My body has reached the ultimate state of fear. The point when it knows it needs to listen to my brain and get the hell out of here but physically can't move. The point where my heart is racing faster than a Nascar at Daytona Beach.

Think.

My brain somehow manages to formulate a cohesive thought over all else. It forces my lungs to inflate enough for me to suck in the air my body was suddenly lacking. I hadn't even known I was holding my breath.

Think. Think, Sloane. Think.

It keeps repeating those words over and over again like a mantra as I breathe deeply through my nose and out slowly through my mouth. It's a trick Brant taught me one day in the treehouse when I couldn't control my tears and started hyperventilating.

You can do this, Jersey. Breathe. You gotta calm down, baby.

I gasp and look around again. That was Brant's voice, clear as day. But he's not here. He's not anywhere near me. I feel tears prick my eyes. I close them. I need to calm down. I'm going crazy now.

Open your eyes, baby girl. You need to be a good girl for me.

Brant's voice has taken on the gentle yet dominant tone I love so much. The dominance cuts through the bullshit while the tenderness soothes me.

I breathe out and slowly open my eyes. Hearing his voice when he's not even around me… That has to be a new level of insanity. Maybe I'm schizophrenic. Or have multiple personalities. I let out another breath and focus.

"Okay. I need to figure out where I am." Ignoring the pain radiating from the back of my skull, I lift my head and look around.

My eyes have adjusted enough to the dark, but it's helpful that there's light coming through a small window. It's dim, but I think it's a streetlight. It looks like I'm in a small basement. There are a few wooden beams. I'm definitely in the middle of the room. My feet and hands are tied to the beams. I'm spread out like I'm in the middle of a pentagram or something.

"Please don't let me actually be in the middle of a pentagram," I whisper.

I tug at the bindings with my arms and legs, but I know I'm not going anywhere. There's some kind of black strap tied around the beam and connecting to the handcuffs around my wrists. My feet are the same way.

Tug, baby. You need to see what happens. How far you can get. Maybe we can get you free.

I do as he tells me, even though I know he isn't really here. He's only in my mind. I don't care. I'll take whatever I can get if it helps me stay calm. I tug on the bindings on my hands first. It looks like I might be able to get loose, but the cuffs dig into my wrists the more and more I move.

"They're not gapped and double-locked," I whisper in defeat.

I had that drilled into my head by Remy and his brothers. Whenever they talked about arrests they'd made, there was always some kind of cruel joke about how they didn't gap and double-lock the cuffs for the people who gave them issues. The more the people fought to get out of the cuffs, the more the cuffs tightened. One person ended up with bleeding wrists, and they all just laughed about it.

I do the same thing to my feet, but I get the same results. The more I move, the more the cuffs that are attached to the straps tighten. I groan a little at the pain and sniffle. I'm not wearing the jeans Blade gave me anymore.

Or Brant's hoodie.

Or his jersey.

"Oh God." I swallow hard. I'm naked. Completely naked. Where are my clothes? And why am I not with Blade?

Breathe, Jersey. Be my good girl.

"I can't." I shake my head as the tears start falling. "I can't. He has me."

Sloane. You know fuck well I'm coming for you. Don't give up on me.

I swallow hard again and force myself to calm. Calm is the only way I'm getting out of this alive. Instincts tell me that this is Remy. I know if I don't play smart, I'll die.

Continuing to stay as calm as I possibly can, I try to remember what happened to get me here. I remember I was on the back of Blade's bike. He and his crew got me home. I remember that. I remember getting off his bike. He walked with me inside. His crew had taken off and gone home, but Blade promised he'd stay with me until Brant got back.

He did. We walked in together.

It's after that I can't remember.

48

I sniffle feeling like I failed. I failed Brant. I failed Blade. I failed myself. I failed everyone.

Knock it off, Jersey. Now. He's coming. Be strong for me, baby.

My head snaps towards the door. I hadn't heard anything. How did a subconscious voice in my head know something I didn't? Lo and behold, though, the door bursts open, and Remy stumbles inside, nearly falling on his face.

He's drunk.

His cold eyes lock on mine, and I swear I see the devil himself. Only, I don't think the devil would instill this much fear into my soul. I'd feel safer with the devil. Remy is far more callous. Vindictive. Heartless.

"Did you think I wouldn't find you?" he slurs. A sick smile slides over his lips. "Fucking my son, no less. I knew you were a dirty slut. Just didn't know that of all the people you were fucking, it would've been Brant." He kneels next to me, almost falling over me. He steadies himself with one hand placed on the ground, but he still sways. "Tell me, little bitch. When did you start fucking him?"

I want to say nothing. I know that no matter what my answer is, he'll slap me. The question I really need to weigh is how bad I want the beating to be. Do I lie and tell him what he wants to hear? Or do I tell the truth and be accused of lying?

In the end, I choose the truth. "Not until I moved in with him three weeks ago." I wish my voice portrayed strength. It doesn't. It sounds meek and weak even to my own ears.

"I wish I fucking believed the sugar that dripped from those sweet lips of yours." He slaps me so hard that I feel like I'm going to black out.

Don't you dare, sweet girl. Don't you fucking succumb to him.

I keep my face turned to the side but keep my eyes open. "I'm not lying," I whisper.

He chuckles dangerously as he stands on unsteady feet. I brace myself for the kick I know is coming. When it does, I whimper. I inadvertently tug on the restraints and feel the cold metal digging into my skin once more as it gets even tighter.

Remy laughs as he sways. "Sucks when those cuffs aren't gapped and double-locked, huh? They'll just keep getting tighter and tighter every time you struggle. I'd be interested to see if they can just cut off your

49

hands eventually. I've never gotten that far with any of the fuckers I've taken in."

"Why are you doing this?" I whisper. I don't think he hears me, but I'm proven wrong.

"Because I don't take to humiliation very well. And that's just what you fucking did to me." He kicks me again, this time closer to my hip instead of at my side. He nearly falls, but somehow steadies himself.

"Ah!" I don't mean to scream, but the cuffs get tighter when I jerk, and they hurt more than the kick. I can't be certain, but I think they've broken skin this time.

"Shut up!" Remy shouts as he takes his gun from his waistband. My eyes widen. I didn't even know he was carrying it. I should've known. He almost always carries an off-duty weapon. But it isn't until he's pointing it at my head that I realize the mistake I've made.

"Remy, please," I whisper. I'm so scared, I'm shaking. My insides feel like they're all relocating. "I'm sorry, Remy. I didn't mean to scream." I look up at him pleadingly.

"Say a fucking word, I'll kill you. Scream, I'll kill you. Do you understand?"

I nod. "I understand, Remy. I promise."

His hand is shaking. He's getting more and more unsteady on his feet. He leans against a beam with his gun still drawn. It's just pointed at the ground near his feet now. I'm thanking whoever is listening for that small miracle.

"You got me fired, Sloane. Fuckers put me on Administrative leave, then fired my ass. Fucking asshole, Colton DeLise. He should've kept his fucking nose out of this. It's always been between us. No one else. You deserve all of this. Maybe if you were a better person, a better wife, you wouldn't have to take the punishments I have to dish out. Maybe we wouldn't be in this cold fucking basement. We could've had a good life, Sloane. If only you could've just been better at being a fucking *wife*." He waves the gun around carelessly. "Did you know my lawyer wants me to plead guilty to domestic violence and take a damn plea to avoid jail?" He laughs. "Fuck that. You're going to tell them what a lying bitch you are. The charges are going to be dropped. Right, Sloane?"

I stare at him in disbelief, but I don't dare say anything other than the one word he wants. "Yes."

50

"You got me in this mess instead of just taking it like you should have. You knew you deserved that. You deserved everything you got."

"What the fuck do you mean she's not here?"

Brant...? It can't be. My mouth opens to scream, but then I remember Remy and the gun.

"She's not here, Brant. As soon as I followed her in, I was hit fucking hard in the back of the head. When I came to, she was gone. I called everyone back immediately, texted you, and called Colton in. Everyone just got here right before you did."

"Fuck! Fuck, Blade!" Brant yells. My heart breaks. He's so close, but I can't reach him. I can't scream for him. He sounds so pissed, so broken.

"Dude, we'll find her." That sounds like Drake. "She can't be far."

"Not a word," Remy hisses. He quickly walks towards the small window, gun in hand, but he's so drunk that he trips over his own feet. Limbs flailing, Remy crashes hard headfirst into a wall. His body crumples to the floor as he groans.

"Please hear me. Please, Brant." I scream as loudly as I can, hoping against all hope that Remy is knocked unconscious and not about to shoot me.

And that Brant can hear me from the basement of the abandoned house next door...

Chapter Eight

☾⋆ Brant ⋆☾

I run my fingers through my hair and tug as I think. "Fucking hell. He has her. No fucking way he doesn't. I shouldn't have left her."

"You can't do this to yourself, Brant." Xavier puts his hand on my shoulder.

"She's fucking g-" I cut myself as we all freeze at a loud scream. We start looking around for the source. We hear another loud as fuck scream that pierces the still night. "Tell me I'm not the only one who heard that."

"Nope. Female scream," Colton says as he points to the abandoned house next to the one we rent. "Who lives there?"

"No one," Sterling responds.

I start running towards the house, but Kody and Xavier physically pull back. "Dude. No. Let them handle it," Kody growls as he strains to keep me in his hold.

"Fuck that! If she's down there, I'm going to get her!" I break free, but Blade pushes me right back into Kody and Xavier.

"No," he rumbles.

"Blade. Grab some guys. On me," Colton commands as he heads for the house with his gun drawn.

"You're staying. You don't know what the fuck is in there." Blade nods at a couple of his guys as Kody and Xavier keep a good grip on my arms. The rest of his men surround the house. It takes me a second to realize it's because they're blocking exits in case my father escapes.

Sterling takes Blade's place. "You know damn well you can't go in there. No matter how much you want to. You don't have the training. You don't know what you're going to face. Leave it to them. They'll get her out."

I glare as I shake Kody and Xavier off, but I know they're right. "Mother fuck." I put my hands on my knees as I bend. "Oh fuck, I'm gonna be sick." So many thoughts are racing through my head. What's he doing to her down there? What made her scream like that?

Xavier kneels next to me and rubs my back. "Look at me, bro."

"Fuck…" I look at him as I take deep breaths through my nose and exhale through my mouth.

"You need to trust them. They're not gonna let anything happen to Sloane. Okay? I know what you're thinking. But we can't let our minds get away from us with scenarios we make up. You know damn well we always think the absolute worst thing imaginable. Our actions need to be based on what comes out of that house."

Xavier has always been the levelheaded one out of all of us. He's a natural born leader. It's probably why he makes such a good Quarterback. He can command just as well as he can calm the storm raging inside us all. I can tell by looking in his eyes that he's just as pissed as I am, but I can also see he fears what they'll find. Despite that, it's the calming factor that comes through for me most. It's what I need.

We all jump when we hear another scream followed by a couple of gunshots and a lot of people yelling over one another. I take off running towards the house again only to be physically tackled to the ground by Sterling, Kody, Xavier, and Drake.

"Get off me!" I yell as I try to get up.

"Drop it! Drop it! On the ground!" someone commands.

"Ah!" Sloane screams. "Remy, no! Ah!"

"Let me go!" I shout as a burst of adrenaline hits. I almost get free of them.

53

"Brant! Fuck, man. Stop!" Drake bellows as they all tackle me again.

There's silence.

It's too quiet.

How can it go from screaming and chaos to absolute silence so quickly? All I can hear is my own breathing; my own heart pounding. My nails dig into the grass beneath me. I'm trembling, but we're all focused on the house. They know if they let me up, they won't be able to stop me from running for it, so they keep me pinned. I can't even deny that the comfort I'm getting from them right now, on the ground or not, is what I need. Without it, I don't know where the fuck I'd be or what I'd be doing.

Ever so slowly, they each start to move off me, but no one strays too far, and I don't dare get off the ground. I'll never admit it, but the only thing keeping me from tearing after Colton and Blade the second each of my cousins move, still staying on their knees, is the soft ground I'm squeezing in a death grip beneath me. My eyes are fixated on the house. My heart is thundering in my ears.

Finally, after what seems like a literal eternity, I see movement. Blade is carrying a completely naked Sloane in his arms.

I can see the blood from here.

My heart stops beating all together.

My lungs deflate completely.

My vision starts to darken around the edges as black spots begin appearing in front of me.

I want to inhale. I want to breathe in the fresh air around me, but I can't. I can't physically force myself to do it.

Sloane.

Oh my fuck. Slone...

My body trembles more violently. Despite the lack of oxygen coursing through my blood, my grip on the grass tightens even more. I can feel the dirt pushing underneath my short nails. I feel the nails bending back with the pressure, but I don't give a fuck.

Sloane.

I watch Blade's every move as he walks towards me. My eyes beg him for answers. I can't look at her. She's limp. Lifeless.

"Breathe, you asshole!" Drake cuts through the fighter jet in my head as he slaps my back. "Brant! Take a damn breath!"

The feel of his hand hitting my back forces me to inhale the air I need. The jerk it causes my body to experience makes my eyes snap to Sloane. The last place I needed them to fall, but as Blade kneels in front of me with her in his arms, I can't take them off her.

"She's okay," Blade rumbles. "She was knocked out when I threw her to the ground after Remy started shooting."

"Jesus Christ…" I swallow hard and sit up. I reach for her. When Blade hands her to me, I hug her as tightly as possible. "Fuck, Sloane. Wake up for me, baby." I look her over as Blade covers her with his leather jacket. She remains still. "Blade, tell me what to do, man."

"Take her home. One of my guys already called a doctor. He'll be here soon to look her over, but she needs you. Just you. She'll wake up scared out of her mind. Remy was shooting at her. She has no idea what happened after she hit her head. To her, she'll still think she's being shot at."

I nod and start to stand, when my eyes fall on Colton. He's coming out of the house with my father cuffed and looking a lot worse for the wear. Suddenly, I see nothing but red. This is way beyond me walking in on him while he's gripping her arm or talking shit to her. It's more than his asshole brothers leering at her.

He tried to kill her.

I let out a low growl. There's a war raging inside me. Give my Sloane to Blade and kill my father with my bare hands, or hold my girl tight.

In the end, the anger wins. The need to give my father a taste of his own medicine and avenge my girl is overpowering. I almost throw Sloane into Blade's arms but manage to keep myself in check. When he has her, I'm on my feet.

"Oh fuck," Sterling says. I don't need to look behind me to know he's following me. I can feel him and Xavier jump to their feet. "He's gonna fucking kill him."

"I just might," I growl dangerously. My hands are around my father's neck before anyone, including Colton, has time to stop me. "Motherfucker! Did you think I'd let this shit slide? Huh?" I slam him against the house hard enough to make him both gasp and groan.

"Let go, son," he rasps.

I narrow my eyes in a vicious glare and tighten my grip. "Who the hell do you think you are? You're not above the damn law! You honestly think you're getting away with what you've done? Are you that fucking cocky and dense?"

He starts making choking noises, but I don't care. "No...," he rasps.

I slam him against the side of the house again. "You know, if I gave the command right now, Blade would happily take your ass to his compound," I growl."

The fucker has the decency to at least look scared. His eyes flick to Blade and scan his crew. "Brant..." It's barely above a whisper this time.

His hands are cuffed behind his back. There's no way he can fight me enough to get me off him. He's tried kicking me a couple of times, but it's not hard to sidestep his drunk ass. Not like they'd hurt anyway. He's getting weaker and weaker the more he struggles against my hold.

"One word. It would be all over for you. They'd never find your fucking body. And I bet you they could torture you so badly that you'd be begging for the devil to save you. Satan himself would be more forgiving of your sins."

"Brant...," he gurgles. His eyes are starting to bulge.

Still, I don't let go. "They could make you pay for every word. Every fucking mark you put on my girl. Yeah. Mine. My girl. She's been mine since the fucking second I met her. You know it. I know it. Everyone here knows it. How's it feel, pops? How's it feel knowing your son is the one fucking the woman you married? That it's my bed she's crawling into now, huh? How's it feel knowing I'm the one giving her the life she deserves? The one she dreamed of that you stripped from her?"

"Brant. Let go, man," Colton says as his hand falls on my arm. "Let me take care of this. Come on. Let go. I'd love to watch you kill the fucker, but I have a better idea." His grip tightens. I don't even know how his voice is cutting through the danger coursing through me. "Let go. Come on."

Slowly, I release my grip. "Remember this day. Remember how fucking lucky you are."

"Cops don't do well in prison, Brant," Colton says as he takes my dad's arm holding him up before he can slump to the ground. "The torture the Viper's Venom would give him would be vicious and fucked up, I'm sure. But think about it from my perspective. He'll get some level of that every single day for the rest of his life. He's going down for attempted murder. That's about twenty years, but he'll never get through the full sentence. Men like him won't be able to withstand the shit he'll endure behind those walls. He'll spend the rest of his life dealing with some form of torture."

I say nothing. He doesn't need to explain anything further. I know what he's telling me. He won't get a life sentence by the courts or law, but the life my father will live behind bars will be unbearable. If he doesn't kill himself, the inmates will. He'll never make it to the parole board. He won't get out on good behavior. He won't make it past the first year. My hope is that it's the inmates who take him after they take every shred of dignity from him. After they take every piece of his soul and crush it.

As I watch Colton walk away with my dad slumped and defeated, I know we've won. Sloane. She's won. Her monster was finally taken down, and while I don't know what she did in there, I know she played a huge part in his downfall.

She fucking survived.

Chapter Nine

☪ Sloane ☪

Shots ring out in the dead silence around me. It's dark. I can hear people yelling, but I can't see anything. I can't feel anything other than the pounding in my head. I feel like I'm falling. There's nothing but darkness above me and below me.

Pitch black.

That period of time before dawn when it's always darkest.

I squeeze my eyes closed and try to avoid the bullets pinging around me. How is it possible they're pinging? I feel nothing around me. No ground. No walls. Just nothingness.

And I know I'm falling. I can feel the wind in my hair.

I try to reach out and grasp anything, but my arms are too heavy. My chest feels like a thousand pound weight is sitting on it. It has to be the centrifugal force surrounding me as I fall faster and faster.

Where are the bullets?

The voices?

I frantically look around. My fists clench around nothing but air.

Or is it?

I grip something soft. Something... real.

Suddenly, I start hearing something other than unbearable silence. Only, it's not calming. It's piercing and drowns out the shouting and bullets. I feel my heart racing. I should be able to hear my heart, but I can't over the inhuman shrieking.

"Ssh… baby, it's okay…," someone says as something strong and warm embraces me.

It should calm me, but it doesn't. I fight against it. What if it's Remy?

Remy!

The shooting!

He has me!

Did he shoot me?

Am I dead?

"I got you, Jersey…" that voice says again.

Jersey…

No one calls me Jersey.

Just…

I can't focus on anything other than demonic and high-pitched noise. I push against whatever it is that's holding me. It can't be Brant. Remy had me in a cold basement. I remember that. He must have thrown me off a cliff or something.

But why haven't I hit the ground yet?

How can he be holding me if we're sailing through the air? Are we both falling? Is he killing us both?

Oh God!

I shove against him while still holding onto my only lifeline. Whatever is in my hands. It's keeping me grounded somehow. Keeping me from feeling like I'm falling so fast. Like it's somehow anchoring me.

But if he's holding onto me, I know he'll take us both down. I won't be able to hold on very long with his weight pulling me down.

"Jersey… baby, please… Please. It's me… It's Brant. You're safe, my girl." His lips are pressed against my ear as he whispers. Something tightens around me. His arms? Could it really be him? "Come on, baby. Stop screaming…"

Suddenly, I feel like he's swaying with me. My eyes slam open. It's not darkness surrounding me. Slowly, everything starts coming into

59

focus. I'm gripping sheets. I'm in Brant's bedroom. Brant is wrapped around me.

And the piercing scream is coming from me.

I cough as I instantly cut off the howl coming from my own lungs. I feel like I'm choking on my own tears.

"Brant!" I gasp as I let go of the sheets beneath me and grip him like he's the only thing who can hold me together.

It's like everything slams back into me all at once with the force of a hurricane. I sob so hard that with every breath, I squeak.

Brant shifts us and pulls me into his lap. "It's okay, sweet girl. It's okay…," he whispers into my hair as he buries his face into it. He rocks me in his arms and hugs me as tightly as he possibly can without squeezing me to death. "I got you, Jersey. It's okay."

I tremble violently as I sob into his neck. I'm still not fully aware of what's going on, but I'm beyond thankful it's Brant that's hugging me. That it's his arms I'm in; his voice that's soothing me.

He holds me close for God knows how long before I finally start to come back to myself. Like the gentle drip of a faucet, everything that happened gingerly drops on me. I'm not sure it's possible, but I find myself needing to be closer to Brant. He's my safety. My anchor.

"He had me tied to wooden beams…," I whisper. "Spread-eagle."

Brant kisses my neck, but doesn't let me go. "I shouldn't have left you."

I shake my head. "Please, don't… I can't take it… I need you to be strong because I can't be… I need you, Brant…"

His grip tightens even more. "You got me. You got me, baby."

I take a deep breath and close my eyes. Brant's scent centers me so I don't fly off into a dark abyss again. "He took your jersey and Blade's jeans. He took your hoodie. He took everything. I was naked. I was freezing cold when I came to. He must've knocked me out. All I remember before that is walking into the house. Blade was behind me. I heard something, then a grunt. I turned and saw Blade dropping to the ground right before I saw Remy. He put something over my nose and mouth. That's all I remember before I woke up."

"Chloroform. Commonly used to incapacitate someone quickly without hitting them and knocking them out like he did to Blade."

I nod. "Probably... My head and neck hurt, but I decided that it was because I was laying it on a cement floor. He used cuffs on my hands and ankles. He didn't double-lock them. Every time I moved..." I suddenly feel the pain from the cuffs on my wrists and ankles. My eyes fly open, and I look at my wrists. As I thought, the cuffs had cut into me. It causes me to let out a strangled sob.

"Hey... Baby, it's okay. You were checked out. Doc gave me a cream for your wrists and ankles to help with the pain and assist them in healing faster. The lacerations aren't deep."

I sniffle as I breathe him in deeply once more. Instead of closing my eyes again, I focus on his muscular arms around me. "Every time I moved, they would cut into me. I did all I could to not move, but he blamed me for everything. He kicked me a few times, but I don't think it was as hard as it could've been. He was really drunk. It still hurt, but..."

Brant breathes out against my neck before he kisses it again. "You have some bruising, but you really are okay."

I grip the waistband of his sweats. "I heard you. I heard you talking... Remy did, too. He told me if I screamed or made any noise at all, he'd kill me. He tripped on the way to the window to watch you. He knocked himself out. I screamed for you as loud as I could." Tears sting my eyes. "I... heard... you. It didn't sound like you were sure you heard me... I screamed again, but the second one made him come to. I heard you all talking about the abandoned house. I knew you were coming, so I didn't make any noise at all. Not until..."

I feel his fingers tangle in my hair. His breath shutters, but he steadies it. I know he's doing it for me, and he'll never understand my gratitude for that. "When they busted in."

"Remy... was still on the ground." The tears break free, but I don't sob or try to stop them. I just let them fall. "He shot at me."

"Fuck..." His fingers tighten in my hair. It might hurt anyone else, but right now, it makes me feel alive.

"The bullet... hit... the floor above my head. I screamed. He aimed it at me. I screamed again. Everyone was yelling. Someone was getting me free. I don't even know what was being said because it was total mayhem. But I do vividly remember Colton yelling at Remy to drop the gun. Right after he said that, Blade, who had just helped me off the floor and was pushing me towards the door to get out, threw me. I think he

61

meant for one of his guys to catch me, but everyone was focused on Remy. I don't know who shot when or why or if anyone was hit, but bullets started ricocheting off the walls. I know I hit my head on something hard as I was going down, but I swore I'd been shot."

"Thank whatever God was watching that you weren't. I've never been a religious person, but fuck, Sloane. Some divine intervention had your back down there, and I've never been more thankful for anything in my life."

I say nothing because I don't know what to say. I've never felt more loved than I do right now. More cherished. And the love I feel slamming into me from him is reciprocated in every beat of my heart. I only hope he can feel it to the same extent I feel it from him.

The words are on the tip of my tongue. Brant rubs his hand soothingly up and down my back as I curl as close to him as I possibly can. I didn't realize it until now, but I'm not naked anymore. I'm wearing a long sleeve shirt that smells just like Brant. I'm just about to tell him how much I love him when someone knocks lightly on the door before slowly opening it and poking their head in.

Colton.

"Hey. Good to see you awake. I didn't want to barge in if you were still out. Mind if I come in?"

I only nod. It's Brant who's my voice. "Yeah, man. You can come in. She was just telling me what happened down there."

"Well, I'll have to get that statement later on." He steps in and starts to close the door but pauses. Seconds later, Blade steps inside Brant's bedroom and closes the door behind him. They both walk towards the bed. Colton sits down on the edge of it and turns to us.

"How do you feel, Sloane?" Blade asks. He remains standing.

"Um… okay. A headache. A little pain from where he kicked me, but it's mostly my wrists and ankles that hurt."

"It'll get better. The most important thing is you're still with us," Blade says with a grin.

Brant chuckles. "Why are you assholes here?"

"Well, we have good news," Colton says. "Remy isn't getting out. Blade pulled some of his connections, and Remy is staying in jail until his trial."

"If he makes it that far," Blade chips in. "Rumor has it, some guys behind those walls have a hard on for Mr. Remington. Rumor also has it that several guards probably don't give a shit."

"They like those perks you've been slipping them under the table," Colton says, rolling his eyes. I'm not really sure what's going on, but I don't think I really want to. All I care to know is that these men are somehow making Remy pay for everything in their own retributive way.

Blade grins. "Good thing I'm doing that and not you, right, Golden Boy Detective?"

Colton throws his head back and laughs. "I'm trying to clean up this town. And you have to go and fuck it up by bribing the badges." Colton grins. I look between them, amused but bewildered.

"Did... I... miss something?" I ask cautiously. I'm more than positive I don't actually want to know, but curiosity is getting the best of me.

Brant kisses me softly. "Long story short, this all has to do with that big takedown Colton was involved in that my father was complaining about. The one that took out his brother, Buckley. Dirty cops. Half the damn town was in on it. The big gambling ring. All that trafficking shit. Well, the town was able to get cleaned up because of Colton's connections. One of his trusted colleagues got him in touch with Josh Lucinio."

I blink as I think. "Josh... Lucinio... He's the one Remy was saying was a big mafia person? And then Remy tried to get Colton fired?"

"Yep. One in the same," Colton confirms. "Only, I had shit on him and his entire family, thanks in large part to Brant. He shut up. Played like a good boy. Was a model cop to everyone else. To me, I'm way too observant. I've been watching him. He knows it. He's good at covering his tracks, but he's been getting sloppy lately."

"He's been drinking more...," I whisper.

"I had a case going against him, sweetheart," Colton says soothingly. "He's been fucking up left and right with the department, but it's not all. He's both selling and taking drugs that he's been stealing from the evidence room from drug busts. I took down his partner yesterday. The guy who works the evidence room has been allowing him access and covering for what he takes."

"Oh shit," Brant breathes. "Are you fucking kidding? I mean, I knew all that stuff about my dad, but really? His partner, too?"

Blade shakes his head. "Nope, not kidding. And yes. Evidence room guy and partner were taken down. And that's not even all. Rem's been trying to set us up for a long time. The deals he has been making have been tied to us. So, we've been investigating ourselves trying to figure out what the fuck is going on because we're not into that shit. That's not what we do. Colton has been helping us out. We've uncovered a lot of shit he's been doing."

I turn into Brant's chest and let out a breath. "Thank God..."

Brant keeps me close. "So, what's the plan? What's happening with him?"

Colton squeezes my knee comfortingly. "I brought a lot of charges against him. The District Attorney is bringing them all to court, but he'll be charged with attempted murder. The DA will go for the maximum sentence. She refuses to plead him out for anything less."

"But the truth is, sweetheart, he's not going to make it to trial," Blade finishes.

I nod, trusting that my entire nightmare is over. That I'll finally wake up and be able to live the life I deserve. The one I was working towards before it was all ripped away from me the day I met Remy Remington. The life that Brant promises to stand by my side in as I push to make my dreams reality.

But it's the protective tone of Blade's voice with the slight undertone of a threat that brings me the most comfort and peace.

Chapter Ten

☪ Brant ☪

(One Month Later)

I rub the towel over my face to wipe off the dripping sweat as I catch my breath. I don't even have to ask for another one. It magically appears in front of me. Our towel boys are efficient.

"Water or Gatorade, Mr. Remington?" the towel boy asks. He's a Freshman this year. He looks like he's in high school, but he's not. He's a good ten inches shorter than I am and hasn't grown into his body yet. His face is covered with acne. His hair is greasy as hell. He's half my size and weight, I swear.

"Get me a coconut water," I respond as I take the other towel.

"Yes, sir." He scurries away with his head down, but I catch him sneaking a glance at one of the cheerleaders who just showed up at the field for their practice.

She's just starting her stretches near my gear, but her eyes follow our towel boy. I chuckle and stride towards my gear when I hear my phone going off. She sees me and jerks her eyes away as she concentrates harder than necessary on her stretches. She's gotta be under five feet. She's a tiny blond girl. I'd question her age if I hadn't seen her ID. She's a Senior and about to turn twenty-three. She's already been recruited to the Dallas Cowboys cheerleading squad.

"You know he has a thing for you," I say as I grab my phone.

She looks up at me with wide eyes and a cherry red face. "He does not!" she hisses. Her eyes dart to him.

I grin. "Oh, fuck yeah he does."

"Brant! Shh! He's coming back!" she whisper shouts.

My grin turns more devilish as I very much intentionally sit on the bench near my bag. "I know he is." I wink. She has no idea, but I've already made it my mission to get those two to hook up. I grab the water the towel boy brings me as I answer my phone and watch him dart away once more. He's gonna have to get over that shyness quick because I'm about to shove these two together. "Hey, Mr. Lucinio. What's up?"

"Call me Mr. Lucinio again, and what's up will be a bullet up your ass," Josh Lucinio, leader of the Lucinio Mafia growls on the other end. I laugh because I know he's joking, but if it were someone not in with him, that threat would be far more than scarily accurate. "Blade said to call you. Everything going smoothly with your dick of a father?"

"Yeah. It's not that. He's getting what he deserves. I think Blade was right. I doubt he'll make it to his trial. The judge was nice enough to schedule it for after the holidays on the premise that the attorneys need to find unbiased jurors. Really, he just doesn't want to deal with this big of a trial after all of the shit this town has gone through over the past year, and he's retiring come the first of the year."

"Good decision on his part. Gives Remy some time to marinate behind those bars. So, what do you need, kid?"

"Uh…" I rub the back of my neck and squint slightly. "This probably isn't the type of request you often get, but it's about Sloane. Her birthday is coming up. Her favorite writer is doing a very small book tour for his latest poetry book. I managed to score a first edition copy of it. I looked at his website, and he's hitting some small towns with small, locally owned bookstores. He made a statement about how he loves to support locally owned shops and places. Tickets for all of his signings were completely sold out." I pause and watch as Xavier launches a Hail Mary down the field to one of our Wide Receivers.

"So, you want me to get you tickets?"

66

"No." I shake my head. "Well, kinda. I mentioned to Sloane that we could take a little trip if she wanted to see him in New Jersey. They're from the same area, and I found out his wife is the owner of a coffee shop there. I thought maybe she'd like to see her old town, but she doesn't want to bother him. I'm not going to push it, but fuck. I really wanted to do something so she could meet him. She has all of his work. She said she's been following him for a while. She really admires the guy's talent. I don't know if you can do anything, man, but you have a lot more contacts than I do."

"Who's this author? Do you know if he has a publisher or agent or anything?"

"His name is Jason Lago. He blew up a few years back when his first book was turned into a movie."

"Yeah, I heard of him."

"His website lists Kepler and Stall Agency. Someone named Daisy is his agent."

"I'll look it up. See what I can do. Kepler and Stall is out of L.A. I have some contacts there."

"Thanks, man. Like I said, I don't know if you can do anything, but after all the shit she's been through, I really wanted to make this special."

"Brant! Get your ass out here!" Xavier yells from the field.

"I gotta go. I'm at practice."

"I'll give you a call." Josh hangs up. I toss my phone back into my bag and jog out to the field.

Over the past month, Sloane has been recovering slowly. She still jumps at the slightest sound and doesn't sleep unless she's wrapped in my arms, but she's getting there. She's not as quiet. She's even spending a little more time with the guys like she used to. She used to make us breakfast all the time, but she stopped doing that for a while. She began doing that again. We're all happy about the way she takes care of us, but even more happy that she's starting to feel comfortable enough and secure enough to start doing things she had been doing but quit after the attack.

She's also been reading more. She won't leave the house without one of us with her, but she will spend time in the backyard by the pool like she used to. She has a favorite pool chair that she reads in. She doesn't know it, but we all have an agreement that the chair is always left for her. None of us use it.

"Hand off," Xavier says when I reach him. He keeps his voice low. "Please show these motherfuckers how to do it right, or I'm gonna start playing this whole damn next game with just the fucking All-Stars. I'm done fucking around."

I grin. "You know we all like when Asshole X comes to play. Whip these fuckers into shape. I got you, bro." I wink as I take my place at the line.

Xavier takes his place behind the center and scans the line. "White eighty!" he barks. Everyone snaps to attention. White eighty means he's ready to snap the ball even though he's still scanning the defensive line. "White eighty! Kill!"

In football terms that means he's ready to snap the ball, but he saw something he doesn't like and is changing the play. Or just that he's changing the play from what was called. I don't need to look at him to know that I'm the play change. Whatever the original play was isn't what it is anymore.

Our line makes a few shifts. It all happens quickly. We only have a certain amount of time before we need to make a play in a regular game. Xavier holds us to that during practice as well so that we never become complacent. Our heads are always in the game.

"White eighty! Hike!" Xavier yells.

Suddenly, we're all in motion. I quickly run by Xavier and grab the ball that he's barely holding out to me as he turns. He raises his arm like he's about to pass the ball, but I'm already making my own turn and running down the field.

"Brant has it!" one of the guys on the defensive line screams. I can feel them all chasing after me as the coach blows the whistle. We all slow and turn. We run back to the center of the field.

"Yes! That's what I'm talking about!" Drake grabs me in a hug and lifts me slightly off the ground.

I laugh. "Put me down, jackass."

"Bring it in!" Coach Steele shouts from the sidelines. We jog to him after Drake puts me down. Coach Steele grins. "Awesome job. That's how a running play should look, but there are other players on this team. X shouldn't need to be relying on just a few people." He nods to one of our

68

linebackers. "Jake, that was a great comeback on your missed tackle, but be quicker on them feet. You're a big guy. Use that to your advantage."

"You got it, Coach. I'll work on it. I'm still getting used to not holding back," Jake says.

Coach Steele nods before turning to Kody. I don't miss the glare Kody shoots him. "Kody, I'd like to see you quicker on the block. Protect your quarterback."

Kody rolls his eyes as he crosses his arms over his chest. I raise an eyebrow and shoot Xavier, Drake, and Sterling a silent look before my eyes fall back to Kody. He's glaring viciously at the coach, but it's not the glare that shocks me or any of my cousins. It's the underlying desire.

"Sure, Coach," he growls low.

"Well, damn," Sterling says under his breath just barely loud enough for me to catch. I know damn well he caught the same thing I did with Kody, but I don't think any of us expected to see the same glare from the coach with that same heated lust underneath.

Xavier clears his throat as the coach opens his mouth. I'm sure he's about to berate Kody for the tone in which he answered. "Enough for the day. Let the girls take the field. Hit the showers," Xavier commands.

Everyone scatters, not needing any further instruction. It's hot. The cheerleaders are getting restless. I know they have a new routine they want to practice for our upcoming game.

"What the fuck was that?" Drake asks as Kody storms back to the locker room.

"Confusing. That's what." Xavier runs his hand over his face. "Fuck, we don't need this. We're struggling enough. I swear I'll fucking bench him."

Sterling puts his hand on Xavier's arm. "You can't. You know he's too good."

They both walk back to the locker room after grabbing their stuff. Drake follows behind them as he slings his gym bag over his shoulder. I reach for mine as my ringtone sounds. Some annoying as fuck high pitched chime that I've been meaning to change but haven't.

"Yeah," I say as I answer it while I grab my bag and start walking back to the locker room.

"I talked to Jason Lago's agent," Josh says without saying hello. The guy is direct as fuck, and I love it. "Sweet girl. She's booking a couple

69

more signings for him. One somewhere on the coast, per his wife's request. The other in Brystone Springs on Sloane's birthday. I got you both tickets. And since you wanted to make this really special for her, his agent will be sending you a little something with the tickets. Rare. I hope she likes it."

"What is it?" I ask, furrowing my brows.

"A surprise. Don't say I've never done nothing for you."

I laugh. "Should I be expecting to return this favor?"

Josh laughs richly. "Are you kidding me? You don't know the hell that would rain down upon me if I did something like expect you to return the favor. No, man. This one's on me. Your girl deserves it."

"I don't know what to say. Just thank you."

"Really. It's no problem. Have fun."

"We will." I pause a second. "Hey, how do you know when Sloane's birthday is? I never told you."

"You forget who I am? Enjoy it."

We both hang up, and I quickly make my way to the showers. I didn't forget who he is. I also know he's capable of digging up shit on people faster than the damn FBI. Probably why he's one of the most powerful men in the entire fucking world.

And why I'll be forever grateful he's on the side of right. It'd be fucking scary as hell if he weren't.

I'm not going to tell Sloane about this until the day we go to the signing, but I can't wait to see the look on her face when she finds out.

☪ ☪ ☪

"Fuck, Sloane…," I rumble as I let my head fall back against the shower wall. My fingers tighten in her hair as she giggles around my dick. I jerk because the vibration from the giggle sends jolts through my shaft until my balls are tightening.

"Mmm… I really love your cock…," she moans around my tip.

"Oh fuck, baby," I push her head back down on my dick as I look down at her. The water cascading over us does nothing to diminish how pretty she looks with my dick in her mouth.

She scrapes her teeth along the underside of my shaft, and I'm done. I feel like a bolt of lightning strikes me. My stomach stiffens as that bolt shoots down my back and straight to my balls. I come before I even have time to pull myself back, but my girl takes it all. She swallows every last drop of me as she sucks and strokes my length.

I fight to keep my eyes open and on her instead of letting them close and allowing my head to fall back in pure bliss. Sloane is far too beautiful as she swallows my come and looks up at me through lust filled, hooded eyes.

I help her up after she pulls her mouth off me. She wraps her arms around me, and I lean down and kiss her. I never thought I'd say it, but tasting me on her tongue is the second best thing I've ever tasted. The first is her. *All of her*.

She wasn't fucking with me when she said she really loves my cock. Since we officially proclaimed our feelings for each other, Sloane and I have found ourselves entangled in each other in some form or another. I'm pretty sure we've fucked in every room of this house at least once, but one of her favorite things to do is suck me off. There are days when all she wants is my dick in her mouth, and I'd be lying if I said it wasn't something I enjoy.

Some might say we're in the honeymoon stage. Maybe it's true, but as I lift my girl in my arms and turn her so she's braced between me and the shower wall, I know that my insatiable appetite and love for her is limitless. I slide into her and thrust slow and deep.

I'm going to marry her one day.

Chapter Eleven

☪ Sloane ☪

(Two Weeks Later)

"Are you going to tell me what's going on?" I ask Brant nervously. He has had me blindfolded as he drives for what has felt like hours to me. I was excited for a while, but the longer he drives, the more the nerves overtake the excitement.

I feel him take my hand in his. He squeezes it and brings it to his lips to kiss. "We're not far from town, but I had to drive around a little bit until the surprise is set up. Sterling ran into an issue, so I needed to stall." He kisses each of my fingers until I'm giggling. I feel him smile as he drops my hand in his lap and keeps hold of it.

"So, that means we're close?" I smile and bounce excitedly in the seat of Brant's truck.

He groans low. "Not if you keep bouncing like that. I'm about to pull over, drag you in my lap, and see how long it takes me to make you scream my name while I fuck you as those tits bounce in my face."

I immediately stop bouncing. "Brant!" I squeak. I don't need to see him to know he's smirking. Damn, though. I really wish I could see him. I love when he gets cocky. He's so sexy. I cross my legs at that thought. Brant doesn't even have to do anything to make me wet. "I mean, I could suck your dick…" I give him a smirk of my own. He knows how much I love the taste of him.

"I'd love to let you, and you can bet your sweet ass I'll take you up on that later, but we're here."

I blush, but let out a squeal of excitement. "Yay!"

He laughs as he lets go of my hand. "Sit tight, Jersey."

I do as he says, but I'm completely unable to contain the excitement and start bouncing again with a huge smile on my face. I'm not usually one who likes surprises. I've come to learn, though, that I love *his* surprises.

He opens my door and unfastens my seatbelt. I giggle when his hands trail down my sides to my hips. He grips them and lifts me down from the truck. When my feet hit the ground, he kisses me as he takes my hand.

"Fuck, I hope you like this," he rumbles against my lips.

I can only smile and squeeze his hand. "I know I will. Because it's you."

"I'm holding onto that." He tugs me closer to him.

I hear the truck door close, and then he starts leading me somewhere. He drops his hand to my waist and keeps me close to him as we walk. I'm wearing strappy sandals that I can feel the grass tickle my feet in. I have on short jean cutoffs with a dark blue tank top. I've always thought I look better in darker colors, but Remy wouldn't let me wear them. Brant has no problems with me getting any type of clothing I want in whatever color I feel comfortable in.

Finally, he stops. He keeps his hand on my hip but moves behind me. I feel his other hand behind my head on the back of the blindfold he has me in.

"Ready?" he rumbles in my ear.

"So ready."

He removes the blindfold slowly, almost sensually. He wraps his arms around me as I blink my eyes open. When they adjust to the sudden light of the sunny day, I'm grateful that he's holding me up.

"Surprise!" the group of people in front of me yells with huge smiles on their faces.

I'm completely taken aback. All of Brant's cousins are here, including Dylan, who's a senior in high school right now. Sterling's step-sister is here. She's still biologically male, but she's transitioning to female and prefers to be called a female with female pronouns. She gets a lot of hate, but Sterling has always protected her. So has Dylan, as they go to school together, though Sterling's step-sister is a year or two behind Dylan.

Colton and Blade are as well. Our entire circle is here. I've been isolated enough over the years that I don't have any friends of my own left, but I'm starting to come out of that. It means the world to me that all of these people are here for me.

"You guys…," I begin softly with tears in my eyes.

I look around at the picnic set up. Only there's a table with a ton of food on it and another with chairs around it large enough to fit us all. It's like a cookout without the grill being held at my favorite lookout spot. It overlooks Brystone Springs. There's a river gently running and lots of trees to provide much needed shade to protect us from the Texas heat.

Brant kisses my neck before he takes my hand and leads me to the table. He pulls out a chair for me and waits for me to sit down. On the table in front of me is a package wrapped in shimmery silver paper. I look down at it then up at Brant as everyone gathers around us.

"Open it," he rasps as he swallows.

I furrow my brows. "Are you okay?" I ask softly. I can see his eyes have gotten watery. Brant doesn't have allergies, so I know he's tearing up.

He nods. "I'm okay. Open it."

I turn to the package and flip it over. When I find the edge, I slide my nail under the tape and cut it. Seconds later, the wrapping paper is off and sitting next to me on the table. In my hands is a hardcover book with a plain black cover. In a cross shape is the same shimmery silver colored ribbon.

I flip the book over in my hands with a soft smile as I caress the cover. I love the feel of a hardcover book. I love the smell of the pages. The ribbon is across the title, so I can't see what book it is, but I'm already in love with it. I'm an avid reader. I love books. I love getting lost in plots, characters, other worlds, and far off lands. A book has the power to transport a reader to places beyond their wildest imagination.

I start to untie the ribbon when my fingers graze something hard, slightly sharp, and metal. I gasp when it catches the light and reflects it. I grip the ribbon tighter between my fingers and look up at Brant with my own unshed tears in my eyes.

Only Brant is standing anymore. He's on one knee next to me.

"Brant...?" I whisper.

He reaches up and unties the ribbon. He takes the ring that had been attached to it, a white-gold band with a single white diamond in the center and two smaller sapphire colored diamonds on each side. He looks up at me as he takes my left hand in his. His thumb lightly caresses the back of my hand. I can't take my eyes off him. I wouldn't want to even if I wasn't mesmerized.

"When I first met you, I knew there was something special about you. But I was fifteen and fucking stupid. I didn't have a clue what it was. I misplaced it, thought you were going to try and steal my mom's place in my heart, and I shoved with all my anger. I pushed you so far away, I'm not even sure how I found my way back to you. But I did. And it was the best thing I've ever done. When I started to realize what I was feeling was a crush, it scared the shit out of me. Then, it started turning to lust, followed by so much more. And now, I'm so far off the edge in love with you that I know I'm never coming back from it. I need you in my life. I need your love. I need you, Jersey. I love you more than I did yesterday. I know I'll love you more than I ever thought I could tomorrow and each day after. Marry me. I don't care it's only been a couple of months since we've been together. You know we've loved each other far longer than that. Marry me."

The love that shines through his beautiful dark eyes at me, *for me*, is overwhelming, but it feels so right. Like this is where we were both always meant to be.

I nod. "I'd marry you yesterday if you asked me to," I whisper.

Brant's smile could rival the sun. He slips the ring on my finger and stands, pulling me with him. His lips meet mine in a kiss that makes my toes curl. He wraps his arms around me and lifts me as he deepens the kiss. I wrap my arms around his shoulders and legs around his waist as he spins me around.

As I lose myself in Brant and our own little world, the applause and whistles become distant. When his tongue plunges into my mouth, everything and everyone is forgotten.

☾ ☾ ☾

"How the hell does that guy look like that?" Brant asks in purely, unadulterated, wide-eyed amusement.

I can't help but laugh. "He has always looked like that."

He looks down at me with a teasing grin. "I made a mistake. We're going home. I don't like him already. Too much competition."

I suck in a sharp breath and look up at him with the biggest, most adorable wide eyes I can muster. "No... He's my favorite author... How am I going to get my books signed?"

I hold up the newest one, a proof copy of *The Drama Summer: A Novel*. Each page inside is watermarked with 'proof copy.' On the plain, black cover is nothing more than the title. I've never seen any book more beautiful. A lot of people are drawn to covers. I never have been. Covers like this are just as beautiful as all of the catchiest covers I've ever seen.

I don't know how Brant pulled this off. He's kept that close to him, but it doesn't even matter to me. This is the second greatest gift I've ever gotten. Brant himself is the first.

"Give them here. I'll have him sign them for you." Brant grabs for my books with a huge grin on his face.

I hold them close to my chest with a quiet squeak and giggle. "Behave." I nudge him with my shoulder, trying to keep a serious look on my face, but I end up dissolving into a giant smile that I'm sure consumes my entire body. "I can't believe you did this. I haven't seen Jason since high school. We lost touch, but I've been following him on social media and everything. I've always made sure I preordered his books. I've tried to go to signings, but they sell out so fast ever since he hit it big."

Brant smiles and wraps his arms around me from behind. He sways with me as he kisses the top of my head. "Well, I'm happy to be the one who gets to reunite you."

"I don't think you'll ever know how much this means to me. We were best friends in high school. I'm so sad we drifted apart over the years. We just had such separate dreams and goals for ourselves. Even though we both wanted to be writers, it was just such different paths."

"You're the best independent journalist I think I've ever met, Sloane. No matter your path, you definitely got to where you wanted to." He hugs me tighter.

As the line inches closer, I find myself reminiscing. While we were friends in high school and did go our separate ways, I've never stopped being Jason Lago's biggest cheerleader. Even when his life was a disaster and plastered all over every single tabloid in the country, I always believed he'd come out of it.

And I was right. Jason grew up and fell right into the almost overnight success he had with the release of his first book *The Brilliant Dance*. It was adapted into one of the worst movies I've ever seen, but I loved the book, and that movie catapulted him into stardom. His second book, *Reckless Abandon*, was also adapted into a terrible movie, but the book itself was even better than the first. *The Drama Summer: A Novel* is his best book yet, though. I even have the poetry one he released not long ago.

While he was riding the tumultuous waves of fame, I was struggling to get into the type of writing I'd always dreamed. Independent journalism. Digging for the truth under layers and layers of lies. That's always been what I've wanted to do. For years, though, all of my stories were rejected by every single news outlet I offered them to, big and small.

I worked for Brystone Springs Chronicles ever since I graduated from college, but not even they gave my skills the time of day. When Remy forced me to quit, it was one of the things I was truly grateful to him for. I didn't have the courage to move on from them. They were my normal and steady. It's not easy to let go of something that provides a steady income and routine.

I can't deny it ended up being one of the best things for me, the other being my divorce being finalized just last week. I've thrown myself into writing over the past year or so and it's paid off. Brystone Springs Chronicles picked up my story about corruption happening in the Wako Mayor's office. Within a couple of days of them printing it and breaking the news, my story was picked up by national networks and printed press, like the New York Times.

"How many more left?" a deep rumbly voice asks in front of me. I blink out of my thoughts and focus on the beautiful woman in a knee-length black skirt and red high heels. She might be a little taller than me, but with the heels, she has a good few inches on my barely five-feet.

The woman turns. I'm not sure of her age, but I'd place her several years older than mine and Jason's thirty-eight years. I recognize her immediately as his wife. I've seen her in some pictures with him. She's even more gorgeous in person. I can't remember her age, but she definitely doesn't look it.

She gives me a soft smile as she turns back to Jason. "Just one beautiful, young woman with a stack full of books for you." She slides a cup his way. I don't need to know what's in it. I know his wife is the owner of a coffee shop back home. She's been keeping the snack table stocked with delicious treats all night and making sure people have coffee, tea, or other delectable beverages. Jason has always been a coffee fanatic. It fits that his wife can feed that addiction in spades.

Jason plasters a smile on his face as he looks at me, but that smile quickly turns to shock. His blue eyes widen as he stands. He looks even better than he did in high school. He was still tall and muscular then, but he's definitely filled out over the years. He's very much in shape and still wears the same dark t-shirts and jeans that make him look even more perfect.

"Holy shit, Sloane?"

I blush but smile brightly when he says my name. "I didn't think you would recognize me."

"Are you kidding?" He moves from behind the table and crosses to me in two strides. I let Brant take my books as he steps back. Jason wraps me in a tight hug and lifts me off the ground. I laugh as I hug him back. It's just like we slipped right back into old times. "I just read your article on Wako. When I saw we were coming to Brystone Springs, I planned to look you up." He sets me down on the ground as he lets me go.

I look up at him and smile. "Really? I mean, really? You read my article?"

"Yeah. Well, Claire did, and we started talking about it, but then I saw it was written by you and printed from the paper here. Man, that whole thing blew up, huh?"

I shake my head. "Oh God, you don't know the half of it. I'm writing another article right now on the fallout. It's insane how deep it goes. They haven't even found the bottom yet, but…" I lower my voice a little and step closer as I look around. It's just me, him, Brant, and Claire, his wife, in the room. Thankfully. "I think it spreads all the way here and maybe even into Austin," I nearly whisper as he bends his head a little to hear me.

"Fuck. Be careful uncovering it. You've always been the best at digging shit up, but don't get yourself in trouble."

I shake my head. "I won't." I glance at Brant and smile. "I have a really good team at my back."

"Well, good. Listen, we're staying an extra couple of days before we go home. I thought we could catch up. Maybe you guys could show us around. Is he your boyfriend?"

My smile only grows as I nod. "Well, my fiancé as of today. He made my birthday so perfect." I hold my ring as I wave Brant over.

Jason takes my hand. "Damn. Nice ring." He holds out his hand to shake Brant's when he gets to us. "You got yourself a good one, man. I'm Jason Lago."

"Brant Remington. And I know." He smiles down at me as Jason lets go of his hand. Brant wraps his arm around me. As usual, I get lost in him as I gaze up at him.

Jason clears his throat with an amused grin. "I'm assuming you want some books signed? Or do you just make him carry around books for you everywhere you go? You know, like you did to me in high school."

I laugh as Brant hands him the books. "You're still an asshole." I smile at him.

Jason grins. We talk more as he signs them. He introduces us to his wife. We make plans to show them around tomorrow and promise to not lose touch again.

As we're talking, though, Brant makes it extremely difficult to concentrate. Interestingly enough, I think Claire is doing the same to Jason because as we say our goodbyes, neither of us are able to keep our hands off our significant others. Despite the fact that we're both glad to see each other again after so many years, we hurry to our vehicles and speed away.

Unsure how we even made it home, I sigh in complete pleasure when Brant finally slams his cock home and thrusts hard. We tried to make it into the house, but we both knew it wasn't happening as soon as his hand touched mine when he took it to lead me inside.

With a recklessness I'm still trying to grapple with, Brant had me pinned against the passenger door of his truck with his dick inside me faster than I could blink. My newly signed books are scattered on the hood where he put them. I don't know how they haven't fallen on the ground considering how hard he's pounding into me.

"Brant!" I scream out into his shoulder hoping to muffle the shout. "Oh… Brant…"

He slams into me again and again. With each thrust, I'm thrown into the door of his truck. I hope I'm not denting it, but I doubt very seriously that Brant cares in the slightest. I tighten my legs around his waist and meet him thrust for thrust as I throw my head back and fall deeper and deeper into him.

He rolls his hips as his lips meet the sensitive flesh just below my ear. He kisses it as he moans low and thrusts faster, deeper, and harder. "I'm never going to be able to get enough of you," he rumbles.

He kisses down to my neck and licks before he bites down and sucks. I know he's leaving his mark. Something for him to show the entire world who I belong to. I tremble against him when I feel his tongue soothe the pain. My pussy clenches hard and pulses erratically. I'm so wet, I'm certain I'm dripping down his balls.

"Oh…yes… Brant," I moan as I pant.

I let my head fall back to his shoulder and make my own mark. I know how hot he is. I know how all the girls want him. I love when he marks me to show I'm his, but I know he loves it just as much when I do the same.

My thighs start to tremble as my stomach clenches tight. Brant shifts just enough so that he hits my perfect spot with each thrust. The place only he's ever been able to find.

"Oh God, Brant, please…," I beg him. "Please…" My pussy pulses and tightens around him. I know I'm not going to be able to hold on.

"Come, Jersey. Come for me. Soak me," he commands.

His command is all I need. He knows I can't finish without it. I come hard for him. My walls collapse as I jerk my hips uncontrollably into his, but it's when I feel jets and jets of his come fill my pussy that I scream into his shoulder. I bite down hard enough to leave my own mark and suck just enough so that my bite doesn't hurt him as I ride out the torrent of my orgasm.

We pant against each other as we come down, holding each other as close as we possibly can. The night sky envelopes us as we stay wrapped in each other.

In his arms, it's like everything that happened with Remy is a fuzzy memory I can't even make out. I can't wait to become Mrs. Brant Remington. I'm so excited for our future together.

And that future is as bright as the Harvest Moon rising into the Texas sky.

The End

Buuuuuuuuuuuuuttttttttttttt…
Are you curious about the sexy Jason Lago and his beautiful wife, Claire?
I totally know you are!
Grab **Through Being Cool** by Jason Handler today and read all about them!

Coming Soon In The Forbidden Temptation Series

The Forbidden Temptation Series continues with *The President's Forbidden Temptation*.

My whole life, I knew I was different. Hell, everyone did. I never came out as a gay man to my family, but I didn't have to. They knew and didn't accept it. And they never missed an opportunity to shove their religion in my face or tell me what a sinner I was.

I took off when I was sixteen and lived on the streets of Dallas, Texas, for a while before the local chapter of Viper's Venom took me in. Years later, after being personally appointed to the President position of my chapter by the President of the entire crew himself, I couldn't help but think about how it was the biggest middle finger I could give my parents.

The only thing I thought was worth loving was my club. They took a chance on me. I'd lay my life down for them.

But then, a brown-haired, doe-eyed angel in disguise crashes into my world and burns all of my walls to the ground. Drake, despite him being twenty years my junior, quickly becomes my entire world. I can't imagine my heart beating without him by my side.

I should really know better, though. Men like me don't have happily ever afters. So, I should have seen it coming when my darkness envelops the man who owns my soul…

Coming Soon!
Keep an eye out for *The President's Forbidden Temptation!*

The Forbidden Temptation Series

Available Now

The Detective's Forbidden Temptation

Other Books By Melony Ann
The Beautiful Dream Series

Available Now

Loving You
My Love, My Heart
Softening Lyric
Undercover Temptations
Captain Charming
Breaking Boundaries
Crashing Into You
Tactical Inferno
Ravishing Our Queen
Cherished By The Texan
Unveiling Our Passions

Box Sets Available

The Beautiful Dream Series: Box Set: Part 1
The Beautiful Dream Series: Box Set: Part 2

The Crane Family Series

Available Now

The Reluctant Mafia King
Sweet Lies
Billion Dollar Love Story
Be Mine
Protecting Her
Dangerously Forbidden Love
His Heart
Love In The Dark

Box Sets Available

The Crane Family Series

The Deimos Trilogy

Available Now

Connor's Legacy
Aryan's Alpha
Kade's Redemption

Box Sets Available

The Deimos Trilogy

The Lucinio Family Series

Available Now

Rising From The Ashes
The Player's Rebel
Encrypting My Heart

Multi Author Series
Piper Falls: Firehouse 49

Available Now

Ignite My Fire by Melony Ann
Regain My Fire by Kindra White
Playing With My Fire by D.L. Howe
Fight My Fire by Darley Collins
Against My Fire by Anneke Boshoff
Relight My Fire by Louise Murchie
Harness My Fire by Ayana Lisbet
Quench My Fire by Havana Wilder

Let's Be Friends

Follow me on

Bookbub

Facebook

Goodreads

Instagram

Tik Tok

Visit my website
www.melonyannauthor.com

Subscribe to my newsletter and get a FREE never-seen-before NOVELLA
just for subscribers!
https://www.melonyannauthor.com/exclusive-content

Join my Facebook Reader Group!
Jason's and Melony's Sizzling Book Nook

The official Forbidden Temptation Series Playlist on YouTube
https://youtube.com/playlist?list=PLGEiD5wbQmDfSjcIbdaBUl79mqR6t
URPP

Dedication

To the forbidden… and the beautiful journey to capture it and make it ours.

Acknowledgements

Brad - Thank you for bringing light to my darkness. I love you.

Laura - Thank you for being a crazy wackadoodle that makes me laugh. I love you.

Jay - Thank you for being my anchor in the storm. I love you.

Ayana - Thank you for being the best friend and PA a girl could ask for. Love you!

Anneke - Thank you for being my ear when I need to ramble. Love you, girlie!

Jason - I don't know how you do what you do, but thank you for doing it and being amazing. Love you!

To the Bookstagram Community.

To my family.

To all of those who believe in me and support me.

To all of those who don't.

Cover by: Carter Cover Designs

Edited by: Alyssa Skaggs

About Melony Ann

Melony Ann began writing short stories and poetry as a child. She continued honing her craft over the years until she took the plunge and began publishing her work, despite having severe anxiety.

Melony writes contemporary romance stories that are full of suspense and a lot of steam.

When she isn't writing, she is loving her family and working to make her life something she deserves.

Melony believes that if her writing can inspire just one person, then all of her hard work is worth it.

Her hope is that her writing allows each and every one of her readers to escape for a little while. To dive into a different world one book at a time.